Seven Brothers

By

Roger Lockhart

Roger Lockhart is the sole proprietor of the book titled
"SEVEN BROTHERS"

Copyright © 2025 by Roger Lockhart

All rights reserved. No part of this publication may be reproduced, distributed, or transmitted in any form or by any means, including photocopying, recording, or other electronic or mechanical methods, without the prior written permission of the author, except in the case of brief quotations embodied in critical reviews and certain other non-commercial uses permitted by copyright law.

Copyrights Case Number:
1-14923754911
ISBN:
978-1-965936-63-4

Dedication

I dedicate this book to God, Family, and Friends.

Starting with God, I was dedicated to him as a very young baby. My mother and dad were dedicated to the church for many years. Our grandmother used to take me and my siblings to church regularly, and when I was four years old, she talked me and my older brother into singing a religious song for the congregation. I never forgot that experience, and that was the first step in my life that I cherish.

I also dedicate this book to my wife of 45 years of marriage, she's always been my anchor and the rock that's kept me on my path. Our children and grandchildren have made our lives complete and meaningful. Our close friends have always been around to comfort us in our darkest times and given us comfort when we desperately needed it.

About the Author

Roger Lockhart has always felt a little different from the rest—a quiet observer of life's beauty, especially the wonders of nature. From a young age, he found joy in the simple things: watching birds in flight and sharing breathtaking sunsets with his wife and family. His love for storytelling began early, writing his first heartfelt piece at just five years old.

One of his most treasured memories is a moment shared with his late mother. In his twenties, she revealed a small, folded piece of paper adorned with flowers and birds—something he didn't even remember writing. It was a poem he had composed in kindergarten, describing how deeply he loved his mother. As she read the words aloud, tears filled her eyes. She told him that out of all eight of her children, none had ever shown the same depth of emotion and God-given talent at such a young age. That moment left a lasting imprint on Roger's heart.

Today, Roger writes with that same passion and sincerity, hoping to touch others through the power of words. His stories are not just reflections of his experiences, but also heartfelt offerings to the memory of his mother and the beauty of everyday life.

Table of Contents

Chapter 1
A Man's Burden

Woodrow Lockhart walked slowly toward the rustic old cabin, his boots pressing deep into the damp earth. The evening air was cool, laced with the crisp scent of pine and the distant smoke from the chimney. This cabin, built by his father and brothers back in '28, had been his home for as long as he could remember. Every log, every nail, every worn wooden plank held a story—a memory. Now, he was faced with the difficult task of telling his lifelong wife, Clara, that it was time to leave it all behind.

The war between the North and the South was no longer just whispers in town—it was real, drawing closer with every passing day. Woodrow wanted no part of it. He had no time for war, not with a family of eight children depending on him. He was in his forties, and his only concern was keeping his family safe. His oldest son, David, was fifteen. By the time the war fully took hold, he'd be expected to join the ranks, and Woodrow couldn't—wouldn't—allow that to happen. The only option was to move west, far beyond the reach of war and its bloody toll.

Indian Territory was dangerous, but at least it was free from the conflict tearing the country apart. As long as they could keep their distance from outlaws and hostile tribes, they had a chance at a fresh start. A chance to live without the looming threat of soldiers knocking on their door, demanding a son to sacrifice. With seven boys and only one daughter, the journey would be a challenge, but it was a challenge he was willing to take to keep them free.

Telling Clara would take all of his wits. He'd have to encourage her, convince her that this dangerous journey was worth it, that with their courage and knowledge of the wilderness, they could make it an educational task rather than just an escape. Many had forged westward before them, following the trails of military wagon ruts, stopping at scattered posts along the way. His goal was to reach Fort Gibson in the Indian Territory, a place he'd heard had plenty of good water, game, and fertile ground for raising crops to sustain the family. But before any of that could happen, he needed her blessing—and that was no small task.

They would have to sell almost everything they owned to gather enough money for supplies. A chuck wagon, strong stock to pull it, provisions to last through treacherous terrain—every detail had to be carefully planned. He knew the journey would be grueling, with hills, rivers, and miles of unforgiving mud, but if they made it, they could start fresh. They could build a new life, away from war, away from the growing fear that threatened to steal his family's future.

He sighed as he stepped onto the worn porch, glancing through the window where Clara was rocking gently in her chair by the fire, darning a pair of trousers. His children were scattered about inside, busy with their own evening routines. Mary, at seventeen, moved between them like a mother, tending to her younger brothers. She was the only daughter, and though she was old enough to be married, she had taken on the responsibility of keeping the household in order.

Woodrow knew it was time for her to start a life of her own, but with everything changing, he doubted she would want to leave the family just yet.

David, his eldest, sat near the hearth, sharpening a knife with quiet concentration. At fourteen, Ronald was right beside him, a smaller version of his older brother, always striving to keep up. Edward, at thirteen, was the strongest of the lot, clever and sharp-eyed, with a steady hand that could shoot the eye out of a squirrel at seventy steps.

Merle, at eleven, was a fighter through and through. His hot temper sometimes got the best of him, but his heart was solid. Wherever his older brothers went, Merle followed. RD, nine years old, had a passion for music, but that didn't mean he was soft—he could kill a rabbit on the run just as well as any of them. Seven-year-old Paul was full of restless energy, always tagging along with RD, hunting, exploring, and getting into trouble. And then there was little Allen, just five years old, a spitting image of his father. Wherever Woodrow went, Allen was right behind, his small hands eager to help with chores or simply sit at his feet while he rested in his old hickory chair.

This was his family. His world. And now, he had to uproot it all for the sake of keeping them safe.

He ran a hand over his beard, gathering his thoughts, steadying his resolve.

It was time to tell Clara.

Chapter 2
The Weight of the Journey

Woodrow Lockhart stood in the warm glow of the cabin, his mind a whirlwind of thoughts, each one sharper than the last. Clara, the steady heart of their family, had always been his pillar of strength. But this—this-this was different. This was not the kind of decision one could make lightly. Telling her they had to leave everything behind, to embark on a journey into the unknown, would take every ounce of persuasion he had.

He had spent hours mulling over how to break it to her. He knew it would be no easy task. Clara was strong, yes— but she was also deeply rooted in this place. This cabin, built by Woodrow's father, had been home for as long as either of them could remember. Their children had been born and raised here, and leaving would mean more than just a change of scenery—it would mean leaving behind their past, their memories, and their security.

But the war was coming, and Woodrow could see no way around it. The whispers in town had grown louder, the rumors more frequent. And soon, it wouldn't just be whispers—it would be real. They would be expected to send their sons to fight. But Woodrow couldn't let that happen. He couldn't allow his boys—David, Ronald, and the others—to be torn away from the family to become pawns in someone else's war.

The answer, as hard as it was to admit, was westward.

"Clara," Woodrow began, his voice steady but full of the weight of his words. "I've been thinking about the only way we can keep our family safe. And I believe the time has come for us to leave this place. We need to go west. To the Indian Territory."

She turned to him then, her brow furrowing slightly. She had known that something had been troubling him, but this—this was unexpected.

"West?" Clara repeated slowly as if tasting the word, trying to grasp its meaning. "What do you mean, Woodrow? Leave everything behind?"

He nodded, his heart heavy. "Yes, Clara. It's the only chance we have. We've heard the stories. The soldiers will come, sooner or later. And I can't let them take our sons. I can't let them take David."

Clara's face softened, but her gaze grew distant as if she were picturing the life they had built here.

"I know the rumors. But the West—it's dangerous, Woodrow. I've heard tales of outlaws and hostile tribes. It's not a safe place."

"I know," he said, his voice firm with the conviction of a man who had no other choice. "But there are others who've made the journey, Clara. People just like us. They've forged ahead, following the trails of military wagons, stopping at posts along the way. They've made new lives for themselves. If they can do it, so can we."

Clara's eyes met his, a flicker of uncertainty in her gaze. "You're asking us to follow in their footsteps? To leave everything we know, our friends, our family, and journey into the wilderness?"

He nodded again, more determined this time.

"We have to, Clara. It's not just about survival—it's about giving our family a chance at something better. I've heard from others that the Indian Territory has good water, fertile land, and plenty of game. We could raise crops, we could build a new life there. But we'll need to act quickly. The journey will be dangerous—there's no doubt about that. There will be hills to climb, rivers to cross, and mud to slog through. But with our knowledge of the land and our courage, we can make it. It will be hard, but it will be worth it."

Clara fell silent again, her eyes searching his face for any sign of doubt. She saw none. She knew her husband well enough to understand that once his mind was set on something, there was little anyone could do to change it. But this was different. This wasn't just a decision for him—it was a decision for their entire family. She looked across the room, her eyes scanning the faces of their children. David was sharpening his knife by the fire. Mary, still looking after the younger ones.

Merle and Ronald bounced around and caused a ruckus. And little Allen, ever close to his father's side, just waiting for him to speak.

Woodrow could feel the weight of their gaze, even from across the room.

"I can't make this decision alone," he said, his voice softer now.

"I need your blessing, Clara. We'll have to sell almost everything we own. The house, the tools, the livestock—everything. We'll need to buy supplies, a chuck wagon, and stock to pull it. The journey is going to be long and hard, and it won't be easy. But we'll make it. We have to."

Clara's expression softened, and she stepped toward him, placing a hand gently on his arm.

"And what about the children? What about Mary? She's almost of age to marry, and you're asking her to leave her life behind, too."

"I know," Woodrow said.

"But Mary's strong. And if we don't do this, we risk losing them all. The war will come for us, Clara. And I can't let that happen."

Her eyes searched his, the silent communication between them speaking volumes. She knew he was right. She knew he had no other choice. But that didn't make it any easier.

"And you think the Indian Territory will be any better?"

"I do," Woodrow said.

"The people who've made it there say it's a good place to start over. The land's fertile, the water's good, and there's a game to be had. If we can get there, we can build something new—a future for all of us."

Clara let out a long breath, her gaze shifting once more to the window, where the last light of day was slipping below the horizon. The future was uncertain, but one thing was clear: the time to act was now.

"Alright, Woodrow," she said finally, her voice steady. "We'll do it. We'll go west. Together."

He felt a rush of relief flood through him, and he pulled her into a tight embrace. "Thank you, Clara. I promise you— this will be worth it."

But even as he spoke the words, he knew there was still much to be done. They would have to sell everything they had, gather supplies, and find the right stock for the wagons. The journey would be long and difficult, but with Clara by his side, he felt they could face whatever lay ahead. Together, they would forge a new life.

Chapter 3
The Echoes of the Past

Woodrow adjusted his favorite hickory chair, the very one his grandpa had handcrafted back when he and Clara first got married. It creaked slightly as he settled in, the familiar sound wrapping around him like an old friend. The cabin, dimly lit by the soft glow of the lanterns, felt warm and safe, filled with the rich aroma of venison stew simmering over the hearth. The air carried the comforting scent of homemade cornbread, fresh from the skillet, its golden crust still steaming on his plate.

With everyone gathered around the table, Woodrow cleared his throat. "Lower your heads for a prayer." His voice, though steady, carried the weight of the decision they had made—to leave behind the only home they had ever known. As he bowed his head, the words of grace flowed from his lips, but his mind drifted, carried away by memories of his youth, of his father, and of the towering man who had shaped their family's legacy.

He could still see himself as a young boy, sitting at his father's feet, wide-eyed with wonder, listening to tales of his grandfather. His dad's voice, rich and deep, wove stories like a weaver spinning cloth, each word full of life. "Son," his father would say, "Your granddaddy was a giant of a man—stood seven feet tall and had a voice that could shake the heavens like a summer storm rolling over the hills."

Woodrow had clung to every word, his heart pounding with the thrill of hearing about the man who had come before him. He remembered one story in particular, a tale that had been told and retold so many times it had almost taken on a life of its own.

His grandpa, a traveling preacher, had been gone for two weeks at a revival. When he finally rode back home, his massive frame atop a horse just as enormous, he was weary but eager to see his family. As he approached the cabin, his sharp eyes spotted something unusual—his fourteen-year-old daughter, Sally, sitting on the porch, her small hand clasped in that of a boy he did not recognize.

It had always been hard for Grandma to keep track of all thirteen of their children, but Grandpa was another story. He took notice of everything, and what he saw did not sit well with him.

Dismounting in one swift motion, his boots hit the ground with a heavy thud. The boy, sensing the shifting air, tensed, his eyes darting toward the path as if measuring his chances of escape. But before he could even twitch, Grandpa's voice rumbled from deep within his chest, a warning before the storm. "Who are you? Why are you here with my little Sally?"

The boy swallowed hard, his feet already itching to run, but Grandpa was faster. His large hand reached for the nearest hickory limb, snapping it from the tree with ease. In one smooth motion, he grabbed the boy by the scruff of his neck, lifting him off the ground as if he weighed no more than a sack of grain.

"Boy, you best listen close," Grandpa's voice boomed. "You don't ever—never—come to my house without my permission. Do you understand?"

The boy, his bare feet dangling helplessly, could do nothing but nod, fear widening his eyes. Grandpa did not wait for further acknowledgment. With a switch crack across the backside, he sent the boy on his way, his words following him like rolling thunder.

"Never, never come to my house without my permission! Ever!"

Woodrow could almost hear his own childish laughter echoing in the background of that memory. He had hung on to every word his father told him, painting a picture in his mind of the great man his grandfather had been—a man of unshakable strength, unwavering values, and a deep love for his family.

A sharp nudge to his arm pulled Woodrow back to the present. Clara's knowing eyes met his, a small smile playing on her lips. "You were gone for a moment there," she murmured.

Woodrow chuckled softly, shaking his head.

"Just remembering."

David, who had been listening intently, set his spoon down and leaned in. "Tell us, Pa. What were you thinking about?"

Woodrow looked around the table, at the faces of his children, the same bloodline that carried the legacy of the great man he had just been remembering. He exhaled and leaned forward, his voice carrying the same deep reverence his father once held.

"I was thinking about my granddaddy," he said, his gaze flickering to his boys, especially David. "About the kind of man he was. Strong, proud, and always looking out for his family. Just like I try to be for y'all."

David's eyes shone with curiosity. "He must've been something special."

Woodrow nodded. "That he was. And he always made sure folks knew that when it came to his family, there were rules. And they were to be followed. No exceptions."

Silence settled over the table, not uncomfortable, but thoughtful. Mary reached for the cornbread, passing a piece to the younger ones. Merle and Ronald giggled, too young to fully grasp the depth of the story but enchanted nonetheless.

Woodrow leaned back in his chair, rubbing a calloused hand over his chin. The weight of the future still pressed on his shoulders, but in that moment, surrounded by his family, he felt the strength of his ancestors guiding him forward. The journey ahead was uncertain, but he knew one thing for sure—he would do whatever it took to protect them, just as his grandfather would have.

"Alright," he said, at last, his voice warm but firm. "Let's eat before this stew gets cold. We've got a long road ahead of us. And we'll need all the strength we can get."

The family nodded, returning to their meal, but the air held something new—something unspoken yet deeply felt. A promise. A resolve. No matter what lay ahead, they would face it together.

Chapter 4
Whispers of the Past, Flames of the Future

The family had just finished the hearty wilderness stew that Clara and Mary had worked together to prepare. The warmth of the meal had settled deep in their bones, and the soft murmurs of satisfied bellies filled the cabin. The rich aroma still lingered in the air, mixing with the faint scent of wood smoke. As the last spoonfuls were eaten and the table cleared, Woodrow gave the familiar command.

"Alright, boys. Get yourselves ready for bed. I've got something to tell you tonight."

The words carried the gravity of a promise—something special was coming. As soon as the sentence left his lips, the boys jumped to their feet, rushing with the kind of eager energy that could only be born from the anticipation of their father's stories. Their footsteps echoed through the cabin, and the room buzzed with excitement. It was like the whole world outside could disappear as long as they could sit at their father's feet and hear his words.

Woodrow smiled, shaking his head at their enthusiasm. He loved these moments—moments when the family gathered, when the hearth was warm, and the stories of old filled the air like a kind of magic. They'd heard his stories before, some of them more times than they could count, but every time, the boys hung on his every word. They were hungry for history, for their roots, for something that could anchor them in the ever-changing world outside.

He stood up slowly, his tall figure casting a long shadow across the dim room. At six foot six, Woodrow was a solid presence, not unlike his father, Samuel, who had stood just as tall before him. He crossed the floor toward the corner of the room, where his grandpa's old rocking chair sat beside the fire. It was a place he often claimed as if the chair itself had been made for him, and in many ways, it had. He reached for the pipe and the small leather pouch of tobacco lying on the table next to it. The tobacco was a treat, something he had kept for special occasions like tonight.

He settled back into the chair, the creaking of the wood as familiar to him as his own breathing. The fire crackled and popped, its light dancing across the walls, casting fleeting shadows. The boys, already gathered in their usual spots, sat cross-legged on the floor, wide-eyed and eager, with Mary and Clara sitting in the background, content in their quiet ways. The room felt like it was holding its breath.

Woodrow took a deep draw from the pipe, the first plume of smoke rising in graceful tendrils toward the ceiling. He let it linger, closing his eyes for a moment, lost in the flickering light of the flames. The sound of the crackling fire brought memories rushing back to him—memories of his own youth, of growing up with his five brothers in a family that, while large, was nowhere near as sprawling as his grandparents'—a family of thirteen children. He could still hear the clamor of his siblings, the laughter and chaos of it all. And as the warmth of the fire wrapped around him, he was transported back to those days of youth when the world was simpler, the troubles fewer.

With a sigh, he leaned forward, looking at his children, all huddled around him like a group of young animals waiting for the fire to tell them its secrets. He was the patriarch now, just as his father had been before him, and before his father, Samuel's father, the preacher with the giant frame and the even bigger heart.

He inhaled deeply from his pipe again, then, with his voice low and steady, began.

"Who knows about the Indian Nations?"

The question hung in the air for a moment, and the children exchanged glances. They had heard bits and pieces about the tribes from their schooling and the travelers who passed through the area, but this was different. This wasn't a lesson from a textbook; this was a story from the heart of their history.

Woodrow took another puff, watching the smoke curl lazily upwards as he recalled the stories his father had passed down to him—stories of their people's land and the tribes that once roamed it, fierce and proud. He didn't wait for an answer; he knew his children wouldn't have the knowledge they needed to truly understand the depths of his question. He just wanted them to listen.

"Back in my time, and before it, there were more than just us—more than just our families here in this land. The Indian Nations ruled these hills and plains. They lived by different laws, but no less important for it." He glanced at David, his eldest son, whose curiosity was always at the forefront. "You see, David, before the settlers came, before all the changes, the Nations were like their own families.

They lived with honor all their own, and their strength wasn't just in numbers but in the ways they stood together."

His mind drifted as the fire crackled on, a rhythmic pulse that seemed to echo through time. He could still hear the voices of his brothers, the seven of them—how they had stuck together, thick as thieves, against whatever life had thrown their way. The Indian Nations, he thought, had always been like the seven brothers he grew up with. Strong, united, and unyielding.

"I had six brothers," Woodrow continued. "And I can tell you that no matter how tough it got, no matter how many people tried to tear us apart, we stood together. The seven of us—just like the seven nations, or so it seemed to me. We had our ways of living, our own set of rules that no one dared cross. And when the time came, we held each other up, no matter what."

His voice softened with a kind of reverence. The boys were listening now, leaning in, their eyes wide with interest.

"We fought hard, but we loved harder," Woodrow went on.

"Each of us had our role to play, just like each tribe in the Indian Nations. But if you asked any one of us, we'd tell you that what made us strong wasn't just the number of us, but the loyalty. The unspoken bond. And that's something that never leaves you."

He paused the silence in the room, thick with the weight of his words. His fingers traced the worn wood of the chair, and for a moment, he felt like he was back there, back with his brothers, under the wide, open sky, feeling like nothing could tear them apart. They had been a unit, bound by blood and by promise.

As the fire crackled on, Woodrow's voice carried with it a deep sense of legacy, of something bigger than himself—something that would outlast even the tallest of trees. He looked at his sons and his daughters, and for a moment, he saw them as his brothers—each one with their own role to play in the story of their family.

"So, remember this," he said, locking eyes with David. "When you face the world, when things get tough and the storms roll in, you stand together. You protect each other. You hold on to that bond, just like the Indian Nations did, and just like your brothers and I did. That's what makes a family strong."

The air in the room seemed to shift. The boys nodded, understanding the weight of the lesson. The fire's glow flickered in their eyes, and for a brief moment, they could feel the unspoken promise of unity—the same promise that had been passed down to Woodrow from his own father, and his grandfather before him.

He took one last puff from his pipe, letting the smoke rise and disappear into the night air. Then, he smiled softly, as if closing the chapter on an old story.

"Alright, boys. Time to get some sleep. Tomorrow, we begin our journey."

And with that, the story was done. But the lesson had only just begun.

Chapter 5
A New Beginning

David was the first to raise his hand, so quick and so high that it seemed as though he were reaching for a star—his fingers stretched toward the heavens, full of youthful energy and excitement. Woodrow's eyes caught the motion instantly, a soft smile tugging at the corners of his lips as he nodded toward his son. David had always been quick to ask questions, to seek answers, and it pleased Woodrow to see the boy so eager to learn, especially tonight when the fire's glow danced across the room like a living thing.

"Go on, David," Woodrow said, his deep voice rich with affection and encouragement. "What do you know about the Indian Territory?"

David stood up, his legs long and lanky like a young colt, eyes shining in the firelight. He glanced around at his brothers and sister, who were perched quietly around him, waiting in silence. The stillness in the room seemed to amplify the crackling of the fire, and David's voice, steady and sure, filled the space between them.

"Pa," he began, his voice carrying the weight of years spent listening to his father's stories, "I remember you and Grandpa talking about the Indian Territory. I know it was set up by the U.S. government to place all the Indian tribes into one place after the white settlers, after the pioneers tamed the land, and told the tribes to get along with them. I remember you said it wasn't easy for the tribes, especially not after what happened in 1836."

Woodrow's heart clenched as he listened to his son speak. It was one thing to hear the stories passed down through the generations, but it was something entirely different to hear them from the mouth of his own child, someone who had absorbed these lessons with such care and thoughtfulness. Woodrow felt a swell of pride as David continued, his voice growing stronger.

"The military forced the tribes on a long march from the East to the land west of the Mississippi River, the land that would be called the Indian Territory. It was called the Trail of Tears, Pa, because many of the people died on the way, suffering terribly. Some starved. It was a time of unimaginable pain, and they didn't just lose their homes; they lost their lives.

David paused, his brow furrowed, his gaze distant as if he could see the past unfold before him. Woodrow could feel the gravity of his son's words, the deep empathy that resonated in his voice. To David, it wasn't just history—it was real. It was personal.

"Now each tribe has its own nation in the territory," David continued, "Where they can raise their crops, live their lives, and take care of their families. But I also know that there are pioneers living among the tribes—most of them military families, stationed at forts to keep the peace and maintain order. I've heard you talk about it, Pa, and I'd love to see it for myself one day. I'd love to go west when I'm a man. I want to see the land you speak of, the land where the Indians and the settlers live side by side."

Woodrow's heart swelled with admiration as David spoke, but a quiet sadness settled within him, too. His son's words were full of wisdom, but they also marked the beginning of something he knew he couldn't turn back from. David was no longer just the boy who sat at his feet, asking questions about the past. He was beginning to understand, to see the world through his own eyes, to dream of a future that was bound to be different from the one Woodrow had envisioned for him. And though that future held promise, it also held uncertainty—uncertainty that weighed heavily on his mind.

Woodrow leaned back in his chair, feeling the familiar creak of the old wood beneath him. He reached for his pipe, the one he'd carved himself from a chunk of cherry wood— his grandfather's pipe, handed down through the generations. With a practiced hand, he packed the tobacco and struck the match, the flame briefly lighting up his face before he brought the bowl to his lips. The first puff lingered in the air, rising in graceful tendrils, twisting and curling as the smoke wove its way upward, dissolving into the warmth of the fire.

His eyes met Clara's across the room. For a moment, everything else seemed to blur. Her expression was unreadable, but Woodrow knew her well enough to see the hesitation in her eyes, the way she avoided looking directly at him. There was a quiet pain in her gaze—a pain that had been building since the decision had been made. She wasn't ready to leave. She never had been. She had grown to love the life they had here, the quiet rhythm of the farm, the small community they were part of. And now he was telling her they would pack up and start over in a land that was as foreign to her as the stars in the sky.

"Son," Woodrow said, his voice heavy with the weight of what he was about to share, "Your day is coming soon."

David's eyes widened, a mixture of confusion and curiosity crossing his face. He had no way of knowing the full depth of what his father was saying, but Woodrow saw the realization flicker in his son's eyes. It was time. The time for change had arrived. The decision had been made, and now it was his turn to take on the mantle of responsibility. He had to lead his family into this new life, even if it meant facing the uncertainty of the unknown.

"We're going to the Indian Territory to live," Woodrow continued, his words slow and deliberate. "We're going to start over, son. It's time to move west. To take our place in that land, to build a future there."

The silence in the room was palpable. Clara's head dropped, her shoulders sagging as if the weight of his words had physically struck her. Without a word, she turned away, walking to the table where the remnants of the evening's meal lay. Her hands, though steady, trembled slightly as she began clearing the dishes, her movements mechanical and quiet, as though she were trying to hold it all together, trying to suppress the emotions swirling within her.

Woodrow's gaze followed her, and he could see the way she closed herself off from him, the way her heart withdrew into a place where he couldn't follow. He knew Clara. He knew that this wasn't just about moving to a new place. It was about the life they had built here, the friends they had made, the comfort they had come to know. It was about everything she had worked for, everything she had invested in their home. And now, it was all being torn away.

He spoke her name softly. "Clara."

She didn't respond, but he could hear her sigh, a small sound that seemed to carry all the weight of the world. She turned her head slightly, enough to look at him without fully facing him. "Mary," she whispered, calling for their daughter to help her finish clearing the table.

Mary, sensing the shift in the room, quietly stood and went to her mother's side, helping her in silence. The two women worked together, their hands moving in sync, but there was a distance between them, a space that neither could bridge in that moment.

Woodrow sat back in his chair, the smoke from his pipe swirling around him, mixing with the crackling of the fire. He could feel the unease in the room, the tension that seemed to hang in the air like a heavy fog. He understood Clara's reluctance. He had always known that she would struggle with this decision. But it was a decision that had to be made. It was time for them to move forward, to take a step into the unknown. And Woodrow knew that, in the end, this journey was not just about him. It was about his family. It was about his children, their futures, and their place in the world.

He turned back to David, who was sitting quietly, his eyes wide with anticipation. "We'll be ready, son," Woodrow said, his voice firm, though there was a softness there too. "We'll make a new home out there. And you'll see, there's a whole world waiting for you to explore."

David nodded, his face bright with excitement and a tinge of uncertainty. He didn't fully understand everything that was involved in starting over, but he trusted his father. He trusted that whatever lay ahead would be worth the journey.

As the fire crackled and the warmth of the flames filled the cabin, Woodrow knew that this was just the beginning. The journey would be long, and there would be hardships ahead. But there was also something else—something bigger than fear or uncertainty. There was hope, and there was the promise of a new chapter, one that would be written with their hands, together, as a family.

Woodrow gazed at Clara once more, his heart heavy but resolute. This was their time. This was their moment. They would start over, and they would make their place in the world, just as they had always done.

The journey had begun.

Chapter 6
Legacy of the Land, Vision for Tomorrow

The warm glow of the fire danced on the wooden beams of the cabin, casting flickering shadows that seemed to move in rhythm with the crackle and hiss of the flames. The air inside was thick with the scent of burning pinewood, mingling with the earthy fragrance of fresh leather and the faint smell of the animals that grazed outside. It was the kind of evening that begged for stories to be shared, where the boundaries of time seemed to blur and the past came alive in the flickering light.

The family sat huddled together in the small, humble cabin, the children looking up at their father with eager, wide eyes. Woodrow, though a man of few words, had always been the keeper of stories—tales of their ancestors, of legends long passed, and of the land that lay just beyond their reach. Tonight, however, it was not Woodrow who spoke first. His eldest son, David, stirred with the weight of history, and his voice cut through the quiet like the first crack of thunder in a summer storm.

"Pa," David began, his tone serious but laced with the excitement of a young man on the cusp of something grand. "Didn't you tell me about the men who went west? About how they carved their names into history? The ones whose courage became part of the story we live today?"

Woodrow looked up from his pipe, eyes twinkling with a mixture of pride and nostalgia. He had shared these stories countless times before, but hearing them from his son made them feel new, fresh, as though they were being told for the very first time.

"Yes, son," he said, his voice warm and steady. "I've told you about them—those who crossed the wild frontier and built the foundations of this great land. They didn't just walk across the plains; they shaped history, one step at a time."

David's eyes were alight, filled with the fire of someone who had listened intently to every word his father had ever said. "You mean like Davy Crockett?" he asked, his voice rising with excitement.

"He was one of the men who went to Texas, wasn't he? He volunteered with thirty other men to fight against Santa Anna's army, even though they were so outnumbered. Over two hundred men against six thousand! And they fought until they ran out of ammunition. And in the end, they gave their lives, didn't they?"

Woodrow nodded, his gaze distant, lost for a moment in the weight of the memory. "That's right, David. Davy Crockett, a man whose name is still spoken with reverence today. He and his men were trapped at the Alamo, with no chance of escape. They fought bravely, but when their ammunition ran out, it was too late. They were killed, yes. But their sacrifice wasn't in vain."

David leaned forward, his hands clasped tightly together as if to hold the weight of the history in his grasp. "The reinforcements were only days away, but it was too late," he continued as if recounting the battle himself. "But a couple of weeks later, a man named Samuel Houston and his army found Santa Anna's forces resting by a river. The river was a barrier they couldn't cross. It became a trap. Houston called for the charge, and everyone shouted "Remember the Alamo!" as they rushed into battle, avenging those who had fallen."

Woodrow's chest swelled with pride, hearing the words of his son. David's recall was not just accurate; it was full of the same passion and reverence that Woodrow himself had once felt when he first heard these tales. He had told these stories to David when the boy was barely old enough to speak, and now, seeing how the boy had woven them into his own understanding of the world, Woodrow felt a profound sense of satisfaction.

"You've remembered them all," Woodrow said quietly, his voice full of amazement. "You've taken these stories and made them your own. You understand them, David. You truly do."

David's face lit up with a smile, but then he paused, as though a thought had occurred to him. "Pa," he said, his voice taking on a different tone, one of curiosity mixed with reverence, "Didn't you also tell me about Uncle Byrd Lockhart? The surveyor who went to Texas before the Alamo battle and worked for the Mexican government?"

Woodrow's heart warmed at the mention of Byrd Lockhart. "Yes, I did. Byrd was quite a man. He was a surveyor, a man of the land. He went to Texas long before the Alamo to survey land for the Mexican government. After finishing his work, the government rewarded him with several thousand acres of land east of San Antonio. And that land became the foundation of Lockhart, Texas."

David's voice grew even more reverent as he continued, "So, Uncle Byrd founded the town in 1831, right? And he named it Lockhart after himself. It's still there today, Pa. That's incredible, isn't it? To think that someone in our own family played a part in shaping that land. The town still bears his name."

Woodrow nodded, his chest swelling with pride. "It is incredible. Byrd Lockhart was a visionary. He saw what others couldn't—a land ripe for settlement, a place where people could build new lives. And that's exactly what they did. He helped lay the groundwork for what would become a thriving community. And that community still stands today, a living testament to his foresight and his hard work."

David's face was alight with excitement now, his voice brimming with the same enthusiasm that had marked his father's storytelling for so many years. "It feels like our family's part of something much bigger than just us, doesn't it, Pa? It's like we're walking in their footsteps, heading to a land that our own blood helped shape."

Woodrow's heart swelled with a mixture of pride and awe as he looked at his son. This boy, his eldest, had not only listened to his stories; he had absorbed them. He understood their significance, their depth. And now, it seemed, he was ready to add his own chapter to the family's history.

"You're right, David," Woodrow said softly. "We are part of something bigger. And we're about to add our own chapter to that story."

David glanced around at his younger brothers and sister, their faces full of wonder and anticipation. They had been quiet until now, but the excitement that had ignited in David had spread to them. They sat up straighter, their eyes sparkling with the promise of adventure and the knowledge that their father was about to lead them into a new life.

"Pa," David said, his voice full of excitement, "I can't wait to see Texas. To walk on the land that our family helped shape. To see the places we've heard about all our lives, and to make our own mark on it."

Woodrow looked around the room, his gaze resting on each of his children, from David to the youngest. His heart swelled with pride and affection for them. They were ready, all of them. Ready to journey into the unknown, to face whatever challenges awaited them in the wilds of Texas. And they would face it together, as a family, bound by the shared history that had brought them this far.

"We'll be ready, son," Woodrow said, his voice firm with resolve. "We'll make our mark there, just as the men who came before us did. And we'll do it together. We'll build something great."

David grinned, the excitement in his eyes contagious. "We'll make it ours, Pa. We'll make it a place we can call home."

As the fire crackled and popped, Woodrow sat back, his thoughts drifting to the journey ahead. It would be long and uncertain, but it was a journey that would be worth every step. They were not just heading west to start over—they were heading west to be part of something greater. They were about to write their own chapter in the story of a nation still growing, still evolving. And as long as they stood together, they would find their place in that story, just as their ancestors had before them.

The journey had begun. And with it, a new chapter was being written.

Chapter 7
The Beginning of the Journey

The early morning was still, with only the faint rustle of the wind through the trees and the soft coo of a morning dove breaking the silence. In the cabin, Woodrow sat at the table, the steam rising from his cup of strong black coffee. He had made it just the way he liked it—bold and bitter. It was a comfort, a small but necessary ritual before the chaos of the day would fully settle in. The weight of the responsibility ahead of him hung heavy in the air. This was the day. Today, everything changed.

Woodrow's mind raced through the plans he had made, over and over. He had no room for error. The family's future depended on every step they took from here on out. He glanced at the worn clock on the wall; it was time. The boys had to be up, and the big move needed to begin. There was no turning back. Not now.

Outside, the sun had just begun to peek over the horizon, casting a golden light over the barn where the hogs and cattle were still resting, oblivious to the morning's urgency. The plan was clear: first, the hogs and livestock would need to be moved. The journey to Jonesborough, just ten miles away, was the first step in making this new life a reality. Woodrow felt the gravity of the decision settle into his bones. The hogs, forty-six cows, and five bulls—most of them had to be sold or traded to ensure the family could afford the supplies they needed.

The rest of the hogs, the ones that could not be sold, would be smoked and preserved. They would provide sustenance for the journey ahead, keeping the family well-fed as they traveled west. The chickens, goats, and mules would be offered to the neighbors, an arrangement that, while bittersweet, would ensure they were in good hands before the family left.

Woodrow knew the land—his farm had been their life for so many years, but now it had to be stripped down, sold off in pieces, in order to fund their new beginning. After breakfast, he would gather everyone and lay out the plan for the day. It would be a long one, filled with the sounds of hooves and wagons, the creaking of wood, and the low murmur of conversations between the family and neighbors.

In the kitchen, Clara had just returned from gathering the morning eggs. Her steps were slow but deliberate, the weight of the day hanging on her shoulders. She was a woman of quiet strength, and though she rarely voiced her concerns, Woodrow knew that leaving their home would break something inside her. Her heart was tied to this land, to the routines she had carefully built here. And yet, she never complained. Clara simply carried on, preparing the breakfast with the same practiced hands that had once baked the bread for their wedding day.

Mary joined her mother at the stove, the two women working together in comfortable silence. The smell of bacon began to fill the cabin, rich and inviting, while the bread, now almost done, promised the warmth of home. That old cast iron skillet—Clara's grandmother's—sizzled as she turned the bacon over, its surface dark with age but holding the history of generations. It had cooked countless meals and fed their children, and now, it would help fuel them for the day ahead.

The cabin was alive with the sounds of morning. The boys, still groggy with sleep, shuffled out of the back rooms, one by one, and made their way to the outhouse. Woodrow could hear the shuffle of feet and the quiet grunts as they woke themselves from slumber. Soon, they would be at the table, ready for breakfast, ready to take on the day. Woodrow's heart swelled with a sense of purpose, knowing that everything he had worked for, everything he had hoped for, was finally coming to fruition.

The table was set. Woodrow sat down, his hands steady as he reached for his coffee. Clara joined him, her face serene despite the storm brewing inside her. Mary took her seat too, her eyes scanning the room, filled with a quiet understanding. The boys filed in, sitting down with the kind of energy only a day full of hard work could inspire. They were eager, but there was a tension in the air—an unspoken acknowledgment of the significance of this moment.

Woodrow cleared his throat, standing up slowly, his gaze sweeping over his family. The weight of the moment pressed down on him. He had known this day would come, but now that it was here, it felt more real than ever. The time had come to share the full plan.

"Alright, everyone," he began, his voice steady but carrying the weight of the responsibility that sat on his shoulders. "Today is the day. We start the move west. We'll take the hogs and cattle to Jonesborough first. The hogs that can't be sold will be smoked, and we'll bring the rest to town. The chickens, goats, and mules will go to the neighbors. We need to keep our best horses, cows, and bulls—those are for the journey."

Clara set the skillet aside and turned to listen, her hands moving slowly, her heart heavy. The conversation hung in the air, and for a moment, there was a shared silence as the magnitude of the day's events began to settle in.

"We'll sell the rest of the tools," Woodrow continued. "We'll keep the plow, but everything else goes. We need the money to buy the wagon and the draft horses, the supplies to get us halfway—maybe more, depending on how far we get. We can't afford to waste time or resources, not now. This is a chance, and it has to work."

Mary nodded, her face filled with a mix of excitement and apprehension. The boys, too, seemed eager, though their excitement was tempered by the realization that today, their world would change forever.

"We'll have to be quick," Woodrow added, his gaze lingering on Clara for a moment before returning to the children. "The sooner we get everything sold, the sooner we can begin. There's no turning back once we start."

Clara reached out, her hand finding Woodrow's across the table. She didn't need to say anything; the touch said it all. Her support was unwavering, even if her heart was torn between the past and the future. Together, they had weathered many storms, and this would be no different.

The meal was served, and for a moment, the family sat together in quiet unity. The bacon was crispy, the bread warm and fragrant, and the coffee strong. The sound of chewing and sipping filled the room, the only noise breaking the stillness of the morning. But Woodrow could feel the undercurrent of anticipation, of hope, and of fear running through the table.

He stood again, once more bringing the weight of the moment into the room. "Let's get to work," he said simply. And with those words, the day began in earnest.

The first step had been taken. The journey was no longer just a dream—it was a reality. And though there was still much to do, Woodrow felt a sense of resolve settle within him. Today was the day everything changed. Today was the beginning of the rest of their lives.

Chapter 8
The Drive to Jonesborough

The morning sun had barely lifted its head above the treetops when Woodrow stepped outside, his boots crunching softly against the gravel path. The air was crisp, the kind that filled your lungs with the promise of a new day, yet heavy with the work that lay ahead. He called the boys out to the yard, his voice cutting through the calm like the clear toll of a church bell.

"Alright now, line up," he said, motioning with his hand. The boys shuffled into place, eyes still puffy with sleep but alert with a budding sense of purpose. He looked them over—strong, capable, and ready to meet the day. This would be no small task, but Woodrow trusted them.

He began handing out instructions with the measured authority of a man who had spent his life on the land.

"David, Ronald—you two are in charge of the hogs. Get them loaded into the stock wagon and ready to go by the time the rest of us are headed out."

He paused for a moment, letting the weight of the job settle in.

"Keep 'em calm, especially the big ones. We can't afford to lose a single one."

David gave a sharp nod, already rolling up his sleeves, while Ronald cracked a half-smile, eager to prove himself.

"Edward, Merle, RD—you're with me. We'll start gathering the cows, bulls, and horses. They've got to be driven the ten miles to Jonesborough. The holding pens are just outside of town. It's gonna take most of the day to get there, so eat plenty at breakfast and stay sharp."

Clara appeared in the doorway, wiping her hands on her apron, her eyes already scanning the yard like a quiet general overseeing a well-rehearsed battle plan.

"We'll see to the rest," she said gently.

"The chickens, goats, and smaller stock—those are for the neighbors."

Woodrow nodded, grateful for her steadiness.

"John's coming for the mules," he added.

"He's had his eye on 'em for years, so make sure they're ready for him."

He could see the boys beginning to move, each one shouldering their duty with a quiet sense of pride. The family was a machine in motion—each gear turning with care and precision, their rhythm built from years of shared labor.

Though the journey to town was only ten miles, Woodrow knew the drive would stretch the length of the day. Navigating the uneven terrain with livestock wasn't easy, especially not with the weight of the future riding alongside them.

"We'll stay in town overnight if need be," he told them as they gathered around the fence.

"Once we get there, we've got supplies to buy. Wagon, draft horses—everything we need to get us started right. No time for sightseeing."

He paused and then added with a glint in his eye, "Keep an eye out for the new bolt-action Model 59 Sharps Carbine rifle while we're at it. They say it's the best rifle ever made. Used to be just a military issue, but now they're selling them to folks like us. Could be worth looking into—might need it where we're headed."

The mention of the rifle lit a spark of excitement among the boys, especially Edward, who had been leafing through a borrowed catalog from the general store for weeks. Woodrow let their imaginations run for a moment before grounding them again.

"First things first," he said. "Let's move."

The stock drive began with a creak of leather harnesses and the clatter of hooves on packed dirt. Ronald led the stock wagon steadily, his posture stiff with focus as the pigs shifted behind him. The rest of the boys flanked the herds, calling out commands and guiding the animals with practiced ease. The livestock moved in rhythm, the dull thud of hooves like a drumbeat marking the start of something greater.

Woodrow walked alongside them for a stretch, eyes flicking from animal to son to sky, ever watchful. He carried the weight of their hopes and their sacrifices in every step.

With each mile they covered, the life they were leaving behind grew more distant, and the one waiting ahead began to take shape.

The herd moved slowly but steadily, the countryside rolling past in golden hues. Fences blurred into fields, and fields into wooded patches where the road dipped and swayed. Every now and then, neighbors waved from porches, some with tearful eyes, others with quiet nods of respect. It was no secret what this family was undertaking. Everyone knew what it meant to start over—and how much it cost to do so.

By late afternoon, the outline of Jonesborough appeared on the horizon, its rooftops silhouetted against the sinking sun. The holding pens came into view not long after, and with a collective breath, they ushered the last of the livestock into place.

The animals were tired, the boys even more so, but there was a buzz of satisfaction in the air. Woodrow took a long look around—at the penned animals, at the sweat-streaked faces of his sons, at the distant town waiting with the promise of new tools and old risks.

Tomorrow would be a day of decisions, of bartering and buying and maybe even arming themselves for what lay ahead. But for now, the first leg of the journey was complete.

Woodrow placed a hand on Ronald's shoulder, then Edward's. "You boys did good today," he said simply.

As dusk painted the sky in shades of lavender and rose, the family stood together, dust-covered and bone-tired, yet united by the hope of what was to come. The past was behind them, and the road west stretched wide before them.

They had taken the first true steps into their new life. Now, the adventure would begin in earnest.

Chapter 9
The Deal and the Knife

The sun had barely crested its zenith when Woodrow and the boys reached the corrals and holding pens on the edge of Jonesborough. The wide open space bustled with traders, buyers, and the creak of wagons. After the long, slow drive through the hills, they finally made good time once their path met up with the main road—a well-worn military supply route, flattened smooth by constant wagon use. It made the last few miles far easier.

Ten horses. Fifteen cows. Five bulls. And twenty-three snorting, restless pigs. All penned in and accounted for.

Now came the part Woodrow knew best—turning livestock into dollars.

They'd left the cabin early, and there was still a good stretch of daylight ahead. If all went well, they could wrap up business and get to the mercantile before the shops started closing down for the night. Supplies wouldn't buy themselves, and they'd need every last item on Woodrow's long list before setting off for good.

The boys dismounted and looped their reins carefully along the fence posts, then clambered up the wooden rails to sit and watch their pa work his magic. There was a rhythm to it, a quiet sort of confidence that the boys had seen many times before. Woodrow didn't say much—he didn't need to. The animals spoke for themselves, and the calluses on his hands told the rest of the story.

It didn't take long—maybe half an hour—before the deal was done. Woodrow turned, glanced over at them, and gave a small, knowing look.

That was all they needed. No words, no smile. Just the look.

David nudged Ronald with his elbow.

"That's a good one," he muttered under his breath, grinning.

They watched as their father disappeared behind the barn with the buyer to sign the papers and collect payment. He walked tall, not with pride, but with purpose. This was no windfall. It was a carefully calculated step in their journey west.

As the dust settled, David leaned back and reached to his waist. His hand found the sheath worn smooth with use. He pulled out his Bowie knife—the one Pa had traded a hog for when David turned twelve.

It wasn't just a blade. It was a symbol of trust, of readiness. He kept it razor sharp, sharp enough to split the toughest hide without a hitch. That knife had a history.

"Pa used it on that big grizzly," he said quietly, almost like telling a campfire story, though all the boys knew it by heart.

"Remember when one of our calves got mauled, and the cow too?"

RD nodded solemnly. "Pa aimed right at that bear's ear... dropped him with one shot. Like he was choppin' down a tree."

David chuckled. "Then he looked at me, calm as can be, and said, "Get your brothers and get that boar skinned. Bring the meat home."

The smoked bear meat had lasted them for weeks. And the stew Clara made from it had warmed their bellies through the worst of winter.

David flipped the knife once in his hand, the blade catching a glint of light.

"Jim Bowie used to brag about skinnin' a full-grown boar grizzly in forty minutes," he said.

"Guess what? We timed it. Came in just two minutes past that. Not too bad, huh?"

Ronald laughed, remembering how he'd yelped to their pa to let him borrow his old timepiece to mark the attempt. They'd all gone after the bear like a team of surgeons, determined to beat the legend's record.

David bent down and plucked a single blade of fescue grass growing by the fence. He held it between his fingers and slowly dragged it across the knife's edge. It split clean and silent, curling into two soft pieces in the air.

The boys stared, admiration thick in their silence.

"One day," Merle whispered, "I want mine to be just like that."

David gave a slight nod, tucking the blade back into its sheath. "You'll get one," he said. "When you've earned it."

They sat in the fading sunlight, watching the dust settle and the wagons roll, each boy carrying the quiet weight of manhood slowly approaching. Pa had made a good deal. The animals were gone, but in their place—possibility. Supplies, tools, maybe even a rifle... and in time, perhaps their own Bowie knives, each with a story to tell.

Jonesborough had been the destination for today, but it wasn't the end. It was just another marker on the long road ahead.

Chapter 10
Steel and Smoke

The sun was hanging low in the sky, casting a warm amber glow over the town of Jonesborough, as Woodrow strolled back toward the boys. His boots thudded lightly against the dirt road, and the seller's slip was already folded tight and tucked neatly into the pocket of his shirt. There was a weight to his step—not weariness, but purpose. When he reached them, he gave a short nod, his voice steady and deep.

"Boys, we did real good," he said. "I even sold Mr. Brooks the hog wagon and the two mules, too."

The boys looked at one another, eyes wide. That wasn't just profit—it was progress.

"Mount up, men," Woodrow added. "We've got some shopping to do. I bought four big, strong draft horses over by the barn. Mr. Brooks gave me a good lead on the perfect wagon in town. His brother's a blacksmith—sells wagons and rifles."

The moment rifles were mentioned, the boys' excitement bubbled over. They could barely contain themselves. Since they'd left the hills, they'd talked about little else—new rifles, the kind that made a man feel ready for anything.

Woodrow saw the spark in their eyes but held up a hand.

"First things first. The wagon and the supplies. Your ma gave me a list longer than the preacher's sermon last

Sunday. The general store next to the blacksmith's shop. Fella in there's named Mr. McCoy."

They rode into town, the hooves of their horses clicking against the worn road. The smell of wood smoke, sweat, and leather clung to the air. The town bustled gently, folks finishing up business for the day, chairs being stacked, windows shuttered. When they reached the general store, a man was placing a neat row of chairs along the porch.

"Hello there," Woodrow called out.

"Mr. McCoy, is it?"

The man straightened up, wiping his hands on his apron.

"That's me. What can I do for you?"

"I'm Woodrow Lockhart, and these are my boys," he said, handing over the list Clara had written.

"Think you can handle everything on here?"

Mr. McCoy adjusted his spectacles, looked up and down the list a few times, then paused and scratched his head.

"What's this here?" he asked, pointing near the bottom.

"Glass jars with lids?"

Woodrow smiled.

"That's my wife's doing. Said she was mighty excited about getting her hands on some. Made me promise I wouldn't come home without 'em."

Mr. McCoy chuckled.

"Well, she's in luck. We've got plenty. Every woman in the county's been after 'em lately—canning season and all. I can get you everything on this list, Mr. Lockhart."

"Good to hear," Woodrow replied.

"I'll leave a couple boys here to help load things when the time comes. David and I are headed to get that wagon now."

Ronald and Merle jumped down to stay behind, already eyeing the shelves through the window. David followed his pa next door.

The blacksmith's shop rang with the familiar sound of iron on steel, a rhythmic clang that echoed through the alley between the buildings. The smell of burning coal and hot metal filled their lungs. Sparks flew from an anvil near the side of the shop where a man bent over his work, his back slick with sweat.

He looked up when they approached, wiping his brow with a thick forearm.

"Can I help you all?"

Woodrow nodded.

"Yes, sir. Name's Lockhart. My boys and I just wrapped up at the stockyards. Your brother helped us out over there."

Recognition flickered in the man's eyes. He stepped forward and extended a soot-stained hand.

"I'm Brooks, too. Abel Brooks."

They shook hands firmly, and Woodrow explained what he was looking for. Abel led them around the side of the shop where a half-dozen wagons stood parked beneath a lean-to. Most were solid builds, broad wheels, clean welds—but one stood out from the rest.

"That there's the best Chuckwagon in town," Abel said proudly. "Oak frame, reinforced iron rims, tarp cover, strong axle. Built it myself."

Woodrow and David walked slowly around it, inspecting every detail. David ran his hand along the edge of the wagon bed, picturing supplies stacked high, maybe even a spot for a rifle or two. It wasn't just transportation—it was security, shelter, survival.

They turned back and met Abel's eyes.

"You've got yourself a deal," Woodrow said.

They shook again, a handshake that sealed more than a sale. It marked another step westward, another piece falling into place for whatever lay ahead.

As they walked back toward the general store, the sounds of the smith's hammer resumed behind them—steady, sharp, dependable. Steel met fire, and progress marched forward, one spark at a time.

The blacksmith and the new wagon

Chapter 11
The Dust Behind Us

The early afternoon heat clung to Woodrow's shoulders as he turned to David.

"Go on back next door," he said, his voice low but firm.

"Grab Ronald and head over to the stockyards. Mr. Brooks said he'll have the horses ready with all the lead gear and straps. There's four of 'em. Just bring them straight to the wagon."

David gave a nod, and in a flash, he was off with Ronald by his side, the two boys dashing down the dusty path like they were racing time itself. Woodrow watched them for a moment before turning and walking back toward the general store.

Mr. McCoy was still stacking and checking the goods out front. Crates of dried beans, jars with metal lids, burlap sacks filled with flour and cornmeal, spools of thread, tin cups—all spread out in neat piles like a general preparing for a campaign.

"Well, looks like you've just about got most of it," Woodrow said, standing with arms folded.

Mr. McCoy scratched his chin and looked over the list once more.

"Yes, sir," he replied.

"Just a few more things to go, and we'll have you all set."

"That's good news," Woodrow said with a slight grin.

"If we're lucky, we just might get home before the sun disappears on us."

The two men moved back and forth—McCoy ducking inside to fetch the final items, while Edward and Merle carted supplies out and stacked them carefully near the wagon spot. The bustle felt steady, efficient, almost rhythmic—like a choreographed dance between purpose and preparation.

At last, Mr. McCoy gave a satisfied pat to the clipboard.

"Well now, that's every bit of it."

Woodrow nodded and went over the list once more with him, double-checking everything, every jar, sack, and spool. Satisfied, he stepped back inside to settle the account, while Edward stayed out on the porch, eyes peeled toward the horizon.

Suddenly, his voice rang out.

"Pa! I can see David and Ronald coming back! Look at them horses!"

Woodrow stepped out and followed his son's gaze. Off in the distance, a thick tan dust cloud curled behind the galloping hooves of four powerful draft horses. David and Ronald each led two, their reins firm, expressions focused. The horses were a beautiful tan, their coats gleaming in the sunlight, muscles rippling with every stride.

"Sure enough, son," Woodrow said, his voice full of pride. "Don't they look great? Pounding the ground like thunder and dragging the sky behind them."

The dust swirled around them as they reached the store. Without missing a beat, Woodrow waved them on.

"Take 'em next door to the wagon," he called.

He followed the boys, and together they began hitching the new horses to the freshly purchased chuck wagon. There was something reverent about it—tying straps, adjusting leather, tightening buckles. It wasn't just a wagon; it was their future on wheels.

With everything secured, Woodrow mounted up into the driver's seat. The wood creaked slightly beneath his boots. He took a deep breath, let it fill his lungs, and gave a short yelp followed by a confident slap of the lead strap.

The horses lunged forward, hooves kicking up gravel as the wagon rolled with purpose. They pulled up right in front of the general store.

"Whooo!" Woodrow grunted, pulling the reins and setting the brake with a loud clack. The wagon groaned to a stop.

"All right, boys," he called with a grin stretching across his sun-weathered face. "Let's get loaded!"

The boys hollered in excitement, rallying like soldiers going into a final push. The town around them buzzed softly, but this little corner of the world was all theirs for the moment—father, sons, and a wagon ready for the road ahead.

New Draft Horses for the wagon

Chapter 12
The Gunsmith's Bargain

The midday sun hung high over the small town, casting its golden warmth over the bustling streets. Woodrow stood at the edge of the new wagon, eyes squinting as he surveyed the horizon. It was a moment of quiet satisfaction, one he rarely allowed himself. A few short words to Ronald shattered the stillness.

"Hop up into the seat, son."

Ronald hesitated, his young eyes wide as he looked up at the massive team of horses and the heavy wagon waiting to be guided.

"Do you want me to drive this huge team and wagon?" he asked, his voice betraying a hint of uncertainty.

Woodrow smiled, his face weathered from years of toil, but his eyes soft with pride. "I surely do, son. You'll make a great wagon master."

With that, Ronald climbed into the seat, feeling the weight of his father's trust. Woodrow gave a short nod, and the boy pulled the reins, guiding the horses with steady hands. The wagon rumbled forward, its wheels creaking, and before long, they arrived at the blacksmith's shop.

They had made it.

Woodrow called out to Mr. McCoy, giving a final thanks for the goods gathered from the general store. "Okay, boys, follow me."

The boys exchanged knowing glances. They could sense it—the air was thick with anticipation. Something big was about to unfold.

Mr. Brooks greeted Woodrow with a firm handshake, his large calloused hand dwarfing Woodrow's. The two men shared an unspoken bond, the connection of hard work and calloused palms passed down through generations. Woodrow could see it in Mr. Brook's hands—hands that looked just like his own father's.

"How can I help you men again?" Mr. Brooks asked, his voice deep and gravelly.

"I spoke to your brother about looking at some special rifles the military uses," Woodrow replied. "I'd like to take a look."

Mr. Brooks raised an eyebrow, his interest piqued. "You're talking to the right man. My brothers told you the truth. I've got all sorts of military weapons, ammunition, and more. The military trades me these things for the work I do for them. I'll show you what I have."

Woodrow nodded, his heart quickening with excitement. Mr. Brooks disappeared for a moment, only to return carrying a sturdy wooden box, its edges worn and polished with time. He set it down on a table made from massive hickory logs—logs so thick they seemed to defy the limits of what one man could lift.

The lid creaked open, revealing four rifles, their metal gleaming in the soft sunlight. The boys gasped in awe, their eyes widening like two full moons in a midnight sky. Each rifle was perfectly crafted and had the unmistakable sheen of something brand new—something important.

Mr. Brooks handed one to Woodrow, who examined it carefully. The feeling of holding the weapon was familiar yet thrilling. "These rifles are brand new, never used," Mr. Brooks explained. "I've had them for two years, but the military just upgraded. They traded me these, and now they're yours if you want 'em."

Woodrow's gaze hardened with approval.

"Are they Sharps carbine bolt actions?"

"They sure are, sir," Mr. Brooks replied.

"Two years old but brand new, with no use. My cousin's in the military—Sergeant Major Benjamin Brooks—and he makes sure I get the best of the best."

With a satisfied nod, Woodrow handed a rifle to each of the boys, but Merle, the youngest, looked up with a question in his eyes. "Pa, where's mine?"

Woodrow grinned, his gaze softening. "Don't worry, son. Mr. Brooks has a special rifle just for you."

Merle's eyes lit up as Mr. Brooks returned, a smile tugging at his lips. He was holding something wrapped in deerskin, decorated with intricate Indian markings and drawings. He handed it to Merle, who eagerly unwrapped it.

"This here's the best rabbit and squirrel rifle made, son," Mr. Brooks said. "And it's just your size."

Merle marveled at the rifle, its sleek design fitting perfectly into his small hands. It felt like Christmas in April—a gift far beyond what he'd expected.

Woodrow turned to Mr. Brooks, who was now looking at the family with a steady gaze. "What's the cost of these rifles?" Woodrow asked.

Mr. Brooks rubbed his chin thoughtfully. "Well, new rifles like these usually cost $30 apiece. But since these are two years old, I'll let them go for $15 each. And the squirrel rifle, well, that one's just $5."

Woodrow nodded, calculating quickly. "And what about ammunition?"

"Since you bought the wagon and the horses from my brother," Mr. Brooks said, his voice low but friendly, "I'll throw in 500 rounds for the Sharps and 100 for the squirrel rifle—no charge. All together, it'll be $65."

Woodrow's face split into a wide grin. He extended his hand, and Mr. Brooks shook it firmly. "It's a deal."

The boys stood, rifles in hand, feeling the weight of their new possessions—a weight that felt far heavier than any metal could account for. It was the weight of responsibility. The weight of a man's word.

Mr. Brooks handed them their rifle covers, each one well-crafted, just like the weapons they held.

"Alright, men," Woodrow said, his voice full of quiet satisfaction. "Let's head for home."

As the family made their way back to the wagon, the weight of the day's events settled into their bones. They were ready for what, exactly, they weren't sure. But they knew this was only the beginning.

And whatever was to come, they would face it together.

Chapter 13
The Homeward Bound Journey

Woodrow gave Ronald a quiet signal, his hand moving in the air with the ease of years of practice. With a sharp "Hep!" and a firm "Go!" he snapped the lead strap, urging the mighty team forward. The wagon creaked as it lurched to life, the heavy load and strong horses pulling in unison. The sound of the horses' hooves meeting the dirt road was rhythmic and steady, just like the pulse of their journey.

Woodrow's chest swelled with pride as he watched Ronald take control. He knew he had made the right choice—Ronald, though slightly smaller than his older brother David, was capable, strong, and always eager to meet his father's expectations. At fourteen, Ronald had grown into a young man Woodrow could rely on. He was already proving himself worthy of being the wagon master.

The team surged forward, and Woodrow's mind eased, knowing that the wagon was in good hands. The thought of who would take charge was one less worry on his mind. Ronald had been eager to please and had volunteered for even the most difficult tasks, showing strength and maturity beyond his years. It was clear that his son had the makings of a leader.

The sun, beginning its descent in the sky, cast long shadows across the road ahead as they made their way home. The journey had been long, but it was a journey of purpose, and the sight of the wagon rolling forward, the boys walking beside it, filled Woodrow with contentment.

The other boys kept a watchful eye, scanning the surroundings for any sign of trouble. Their movements were coordinated, their alertness sharp, a reflection of the training Woodrow had instilled in them. They were not just sons; they were the next generation of trailblazers.

The day had been full of work, but it was also full of rewards—their trip to the store had been a success, and the new rifles they carried were sure to make a difference in the future. These were no ordinary weapons; they were the finest rifles made, and with plenty of ammunition to spare, they had enough firepower to defend themselves against any threat, be it man or beast. Woodrow couldn't help but feel a sense of security knowing they had such powerful tools at their disposal.

As the wagon creaked along, the golden hour of the evening settled in. The sun hung low in the sky, casting hues of orange, pink, and purple across the landscape. It was a sight so beautiful that it almost didn't seem real—a painting, hand-crafted by the finest artist. Woodrow glanced up at the sky, his heart swelling with gratitude. He knew that there was something greater than themselves guiding them on this journey—a divine hand that had carried them this far and would continue to watch over them.

It had been a long day, and there was much to do once they got home—stable the horses, clean up, and prepare for supper. But in that moment, as they traveled under the dying light of the sun, Woodrow knew that they were exactly where they were meant to be.

Together.

Woodrow's goodbye visit to his brother

Chapter 14
The Weight of Goodbye

Woodrow's eyes lingered on the faint glow of light emanating from the cabin's windows, a distant beacon that stirred a mix of nostalgia and sorrow in his chest. The historic structure had seen so much—life, laughter, heartache, and joy—since its first days back in 028. It was more than a cabin; it was the foundation of his family's past, the home where they'd built their lives, weathered storms, and celebrated victories, both big and small. Now, that same home stood before him, a reminder of everything they were about to leave behind.

He had promised his younger brother that the cabin would be his if Woodrow and his family moved on. It was a promise made out of duty, yet one that felt heavier than he had expected. Walking away from it now seemed impossible. But he knew there was no other choice. The future lay beyond the familiar walls of the cabin, a future filled with uncertainty, yet tinged with the promise of something new. Woodrow's heart weighed heavy, torn between the love for the land he had worked with his hands and the pull of the unknown path that lay ahead.

The week before them would be a whirlwind of work—there was so much to do, so little time. The hogs needed to be butchered, their meat preserved for the journey. Bacon, hams, and select cuts would be canned, the jars serving not just as storage, but as a lifeline. Woodrow's wife, skilled in the art of preservation, would turn each piece of meat into something that could feed them along the trail, ensuring their survival through the days ahead. The man at the general store had mentioned how women in the area used these jars for nearly everything, and Woodrow knew that if his family was to make it, these jars would carry their hopes and their sustenance.

The cows and the bull were another part of the plan. Woodrow had kept them, knowing they might be necessary if times got tougher than expected. There was always a chance the trail would become too rough, the weather too unforgiving. In those times, food was more important than anything money could buy, and he had learned through experience that having a stable source of food would make all the difference. But despite these preparations, he wasn't without his own resources. Deep in his pocket was nearly six hundred dollars in gold coins—hard-earned, well-earned, and tucked away for the journey ahead. It was enough to get them to the Indian Territory, enough to buy them a fresh start on their new homestead.

As the wagon drew closer to the cabin, the familiar sound of their walker hunting hounds met Woodrow's ears. The dog's excited barks filled the air, their voices carrying a sense of recognition, as if they knew they were home, and that this chapter was ending. The hounds dashed toward the wagon, their tails wagging furiously, as they ran ahead to greet the family.

Woodrow's heart swelled with emotion as he watched the hounds. They had been with the family through thick and thin, companions on countless hunts, guardians of the land, and protectors of the family. Their joy was contagious, and for a fleeting moment, Woodrow allowed himself to feel the warmth of home once more. But it was fleeting. The moment was passing, and there was no turning back.

Stepping down from the wagon, Woodrow looked at the cabin one last time. The door creaked open, revealing the familiar walls, the worn floors, and the hearth where his family had gathered countless nights. It was a place filled with memories—memories of laughter around the dinner table, the quiet evenings spent by the fire, the moments of peace they had fought so hard to preserve. But those memories would have to stay here, in this cabin.

Woodrow could feel the weight of the past on his shoulders as he walked toward the door. The promise he had made to his brother tugged at him, but he knew that his family's future lay beyond this place. There was a new life waiting for them in the Indian Territory, a chance to build something fresh, something theirs. But as he stepped through the door, he couldn't help but feel the sting of leaving behind everything they had worked for. The cabin, the land, the memories—everything that had shaped him and his family would stay here.

With a deep breath, he turned around and gave the cabin one last, lingering look. The light from inside flickered softly, casting a warm glow against the fading daylight. It was as if the cabin itself was saying goodbye, acknowledging that this chapter of their lives was ending.

Woodrow stepped inside, and as the door closed behind him, he felt the weight of the moment settle in. This was the end of one journey, and the beginning of another. It wasn't just a house they were leaving—it was a part of their history, a part of who they were. And as they prepared to move on, they would carry that history with them, wherever the road might lead.

Chapter 15
The Joy of New Beginnings

Clara, Mary, and the boys spilled out of the cabin in a rush, their excitement bubbling over as though the cabin was on fire. The sight that greeted them was enough to make their hearts leap. It was Mary who spoke first, her voice full of awe, "Oh Pa, they're beautiful!" She had always been the horse lover of the family, ever since she was a little girl. The moment the wagon pulled up, Mary was the first to rush toward the animals, eager to care for them just as she had done with every horse they'd owned. After Clara began preparing breakfast each morning, it was always Mary who would run out to the barn to ensure the horses were fed, groomed, and well cared for. There was no doubt that the horses had a special place in her heart.

Clara, too, was impressed by the sight before her. Even in the dim light of early morning, the huge working chuck wagon stood tall and imposing, nearly as large as the family's hopes for the future. Woodrow, with a gleam of pride in his eyes, told her, "It's stacked full of the supplies from your list, Clara. Even the canning jars you asked for." Clara's eyes softened with a smile of gratitude. She had always worked hard to ensure the family had what they needed, and now, seeing the supplies that would carry them through their journey, her heart swelled with a quiet joy.

"Alright, men," Woodrow called to the boys, his voice firm yet warm. "Let's get these horses into the stable and taken care of before we wash up and enjoy the chicken dinner your mom and sister have prepared." The boys wasted no time in jumping into action. They had worked hard alongside their father, and now it was time for the final tasks of the day.

By the time the chores were finished, darkness had settled over the land, the cool night air wrapping around them like a blanket. But the promise of a warm meal pulled them back to the cabin. The boys hurried to wash up, eager to settle into their favorite places around the table.

The delicious smell of fried chicken and mashed potatoes with gravy filled the cabin, and even Woodrow, weary from the day's work, couldn't help but smile. He had been right: the chicken dinner smelled as good as it tasted, and they were all ready to dig in. Clara had outdone herself, as always.

The table was laid with steaming hot bread, golden brown and still warm from the oven, waiting to be torn into by eager hands. It was the simple comforts of home that Woodrow cherished—the meals, the laughter, the togetherness of his family—and tonight, it was all coming together perfectly.

As they sat down to eat, Woodrow felt a deep sense of gratitude. The table was filled with his children, his wife, and his sister, all gathered around, sharing the fruits of their labor. It was a blessing to have a family so willing to pitch in, to work together toward something greater than any one of them could achieve alone. The boys ate eagerly, but they were also eager to share a surprise with the rest of the family.

They had something special in mind, something that had been carefully kept under wraps until this very moment.

Woodrow had not forgotten his family while he was at the general store. Clara and Mary had received new dresses and shoes, gifts that would serve them well on the road ahead. The younger boys had also received new shoes and a small Henckels knife each, a tool that would be invaluable for their work ahead. The youngest, Allen, had received something unique—a carved wooden soldier and horse, a toy that would remind him of home as they journeyed on. But it was the older boys who were most excited about their gifts. They could hardly wait to show off their new rifles, their faces lit with pride as they displayed them to the family.

The gleam of the rifles in the flickering lantern light seemed almost magical, and Clara's eyes shifted toward them. Woodrow noticed her look—she had always been practical and cautious, but he knew she would approve once she saw everything in the light of day. The rifles, after all, were for their protection, a necessary part of the journey they were about to undertake.

As the family finished their meal and the sounds of contentment filled the air, Woodrow leaned back, satisfied. It had been a long, rewarding day, but it was finally over. The work was done, the gifts were given, and now, they could rest. Tomorrow would bring new challenges, but tonight, they had each other and the comfort of their home.

He looked around the table, his heart full. It wasn't just the food that made the meal special—it was the togetherness, the bond they shared, and the knowledge that they were embarking on a new chapter of their lives, together.

As the evening wound down and the sounds of laughter faded, the family slowly retired for the night, each of them carrying the weight of the day's work and the promise of what lay ahead. Woodrow's heart was full of quiet satisfaction, knowing that despite the challenges, they would face them all as a family, united in purpose and love. Tomorrow would come with its own trials, but for now, it was time to rest.

Chapter 16
A Busy Morning and a Full Day of Work

As Woodrow and Clara approached the cabin, they could hear the familiar sounds of the children stirring inside. The air was already thick with the warmth of a new day, and the bustling noises from within suggested that the morning had already begun in earnest. When they pushed open the door, the sight that greeted them was both comforting and busy. The kids were already up, dressed in their simple but sturdy clothes, eager to start the day. The cabin was alive with energy, the air filled with the scents of breakfast being prepared.

Mary, ever the diligent helper, was already at the stove. She was finishing up the bacon, carefully arranging the crispy strips on the large platter that had been passed down through Clara's family. It was a special dish, one that carried memories of mornings past—of simpler times, yet rich with love and tradition. Clara, with a smile, filled a big bowl with scrambled eggs, the golden yolks coming from the fresh eggs they had gathered that morning from the chicken coop. The chickens were in full production, their eggs a much-appreciated luxury in these busy times.

Clara motioned for the children to take their seats around the wooden table. The boys, with their rough-and-tumble energy, scrambled into their places, while Mary, always the gentle soul, made sure everyone had a spot. The table was soon filled with the hearty meal: crispy bacon, fluffy scrambled eggs, and steaming hot biscuits, all topped off with Clara's famous homemade gravy. The simple meal reflected the love and care Clara put into every dish. Woodrow looked around the room, his heart swelling with pride and contentment. His children, growing older but still full of life and love, sat before him, their faces eager with anticipation. They had learned so much, but there was still so much more to come, and this breakfast, simple as it was, was a moment of calm before the storm of tasks ahead.

Woodrow cleared his throat and looked at his children. He smiled warmly, his heart full of gratitude. "Alright, kids," he said softly, his voice steady and reassuring. "Let's bow our heads and thank the Lord for this meal." They all lowered their heads, and the room was filled with the sound of his deep, humble voice offering a prayer of thanks for the food, for the family, and for the work ahead. There was a sense of peace in the air, despite the whirlwind of activities to come.

After breakfast, Woodrow stood and gestured for the children to follow him outside. The morning light was already starting to stretch across the land, casting a golden glow on the scene outside. The fresh air was invigorating, a reminder of the work that lay ahead. The children, full of energy, eagerly followed their father, their eyes wide with excitement for the tasks they had yet to tackle. Mary and the younger boys were immediately drawn to the new wagon, their faces lighting up as they touched the sturdy wood and smooth iron of the wheels. They climbed all over it, inspecting every detail, imagining the journeys it would carry them on in the days to come. It was a treasure to them, a symbol of their new life and the promise of adventure.

Woodrow looked at the older boys—David, Ronald, Edward, and Merle—and spoke with purpose. "Alright, boys, here's the plan for the day," he said, his voice firm but filled with the love of a father who knew the importance of hard work. "You four will be butchering the hogs, gathering wood for the smokehouse, and getting the meat into it. It's a big job, but I know you're ready. Let's get to it."

The boys nodded, their faces set with determination. They had grown accustomed to these hard, physical tasks. They knew the importance of what they were doing. The meat they would prepare and preserve would sustain them through their journey westward. It was not just work—it was survival.

Woodrow turned to Clara, who stood nearby, already organizing the supplies she would need for her own tasks. "Clara," he said with a smile, "You and Mary will need to boil the new canning jars and lids. We've got plenty of meat coming our way, and we'll need to preserve it all. The canning jars will help ensure that we have enough food to make it through the long journey ahead." Clara nodded in agreement, her face calm but full of purpose. She knew the importance of what lay ahead. Preserving food was a vital part of their survival, especially when they were about to embark on a long and uncertain journey.

As Woodrow watched the children disperse, each one taking on their responsibilities with the eagerness of youth, he couldn't help but feel a deep sense of pride. There was much to do, but the family was ready. There was no room for hesitation, only action. The work was hard, but it was necessary. The meat would be smoked and canned, stored for the trip ahead. Woodrow estimated that it would take about a week for everything to be cured, after which they would be ready to set out on their westward journey. There was much to prepare, but they were making progress. And with every day, they moved closer to their new life.

Woodrow felt the weight of the task ahead, but he also felt the strength of his family. They had made it this far, and with each passing day, they grew stronger. Together, they would face whatever challenges came their way. But for now, it was time to work, time to prepare, and time to finish what had been started.

Chapter 17
A Farewell to the Old Cabin and New Beginnings

The last of the meat was now hanging in the smokehouse, slowly curing, while the rest had been carefully canned into the new glass jars Clara was so proud of. Every jar was a testament to her hard work, her meticulous nature, and her desire to preserve not only the food but the memories of these days. Each step had brought them closer to the future, but in the quiet moments, Woodrow couldn't help but feel the weight of what they were leaving behind.

Sitting at the kitchen table, Woodrow sipped the last of his second cup of coffee, letting the warmth of the brew settle into his bones. The day had already begun in earnest, with the usual hustle and bustle of chores filling the air. He had just finished breakfast, the kitchen was now quiet after the kids had gone outside to continue their tasks. As he glanced over at Clara, he gave her a small nod, signaling her to come closer.

Clara, always attentive to her husband's every move, walked over to him with a smile, wiping her hands on her apron. But before she could ask what he needed, Woodrow reached out, pulling her onto his lap with a mischievous grin on his face. Surprised, Clara laughed, swatting him playfully with the dish towel she held in her hand. "What's so important?" she asked quietly, her eyes dancing with curiosity.

Woodrow's smile softened, and for a moment, he simply held her, his mind racing through the years that had passed. "This," he began, his voice low and thoughtful, "This has been our wedding cottage. It's where we started our life together, where we raised our children, and where we built our dreams." His hand gently swept over the table and the room, as if trying to capture the essence of everything that had happened within these walls.

Clara felt a rush of emotion as she looked around the familiar space, the cabin that had been their haven for so many years. It had witnessed their triumphs, their struggles, their love, and their family's growth. She smiled wistfully, feeling the warmth of their early days here, the feeling of stepping into this little home together all those years ago. It had been a place full of love, and even though they were moving on, part of it would always stay with them.

"I know," she whispered, squeezing his hand. "It's hard to leave, but we're not leaving it behind forever. We'll take those memories with us."

Woodrow nodded.

"We'll miss this place, but we're going to build a new home, a new life. And we'll do it together, just like we've always done."

There was a brief moment of silence between them, both lost in their own thoughts. Finally, Woodrow broke the silence, his voice steady but with a hint of finality.

"Clara, I need to go see my little brother. I promised him this place when we left. It's time to give it to him. I'm leaving Grandpa's rocking chair here, along with everything else in the cabin. It all stays, except for our clothes and what we need for the journey."

Clara's heart tightened at the thought of leaving, but she understood. It was time to let go.

"I know," she said softly. "I'll be fine here. You go. Take Edward with you. He's been wanting to go with you on one of your trips."

Woodrow's face softened, a small smile tugging at the corners of his mouth.

"It's his turn. And we need to talk. I've got something for him."

Clara raised an eyebrow.

"What's that?"

Woodrow's grin grew wider. "He's been wanting one for a long time, and I've been telling him I'd get him one. I've bought him a new Bowie knife. I know he'll be thrilled."

Clara's eyes widened in surprise. She knew how much Edward had admired the Bowie knives his older brothers had, how much he had longed for one of his own. This was a gesture of love and care, and Clara couldn't help but feel proud of Woodrow for thinking of it.

With that, Woodrow stood up, placing a kiss on Clara's cheek. He stepped outside, letting out a loud yelp, the kind that could be heard echoing down the hillside. The boys, ever alert, came running back to the house, responding in unison.

"Yes, sir?"

Woodrow smiled at them, his voice commanding yet full of fatherly affection.

"I need you, David. You're in charge while I'm gone with Edward. Make sure everything is taken care of. Check in with your ma and see if she needs anything else from you boys."

David nodded, his chest puffing out with pride. He was the oldest, and he knew the responsibility that came with it.

"Yes, Pa."

Woodrow turned to Edward, who had been standing nearby, waiting for his instructions. "

Edward," he said, his tone softening, "Go saddle up our horses and strap on our new rifles. We're heading to see your uncle today."

Edward's eyes lit up with excitement, but there was something else in his gaze—a sense of responsibility and anticipation. This wasn't just about the journey; it was about the passage from boyhood to manhood. It was his turn to prove himself, and the rifle he carried would serve as a reminder of that.

Woodrow could see the pride in his son's eyes as he nodded.

"Yes, Pa. I'll get the horses ready."

As Edward hurried off to prepare, Woodrow stood for a moment, looking back at the cabin one last time. The next chapter of their lives was beginning, and with it, a new set of responsibilities. But Woodrow knew that whatever came their way, they would face it together, strong, united, and ready for whatever lay ahead.

Chapter 18
A Farewell and a Big Announcement

The morning light was still gentle and soft as Woodrow and Edward began their journey, their horses' hooves clicking rhythmically against the dew-laden trail. It was one of those mornings that seemed to stretch forever when everything felt timeless and the earth itself felt alive with the quiet hum of daybreak. The landscape, still bathed in the early light, was like a painting, its vastness spreading before them. As the air cooled with the fresh mountain breeze, the scent of pine and damp earth lingered in their lungs. They were not just on a journey to visit family; they were also embarking on a journey that signified change—a deep, inevitable shift.

Woodrow and Edward rode in comfortable silence for a time, the sound of their horses" steps the only noise between them. But soon, the quiet began to fade as they exchanged stories. They shared small, familiar anecdotes from their past—tales of their younger years, the trouble they"d gotten into, and the moments that had shaped their bond. The trail felt lighter under their feet with every word shared, every laugh exchanged. Even so, beneath the easy banter, Woodrow's mind was focused, thinking about the task ahead, the news he needed to share with his younger brother, and the responsibility of what that news meant for their entire family.

After a time, Woodrow reached under his coat, feeling the smooth, familiar bundle wrapped in deer skin. It had been there for hours, nestled against his side like a secret, something he'd been holding onto with great care. As the morning sun broke through the trees, Woodrow pulled it out and held it out to Edward.

"Here, son. This is for you."

Edward's eyes widened with curiosity, a spark of excitement lighting up his face. He took the bundle carefully, his fingers trembling ever so slightly as he began to unravel the deer skin. The slow, deliberate unwrapping only heightened the tension between them, and Woodrow couldn't help but watch with a quiet sense of pride as Edward's hands revealed the prize. When the Bowie knife appeared, Edward's expression shifted in an instant—from anticipation to sheer exhilaration. His mouth dropped open in surprise, and he let out a loud "Woo-wee!" that echoed through the mountain valleys. The sound seemed to reverberate through the earth, filling the air with the joy and excitement of the moment. It was as if the mountains themselves were celebrating with them, the very earth joining in their moment of happiness.

Woodrow couldn't help but grin, a deep satisfaction settling in his chest. He had been planning this for months. The knife was more than just a blade—it was a symbol of growing up, of taking on more responsibility, of entering the world as a man among men. Edward had envied his older brothers' knives for years, watching as they performed tricks and took on challenges. Now, it was his turn. This moment marked the beginning of something new for him, something Woodrow had hoped to pass down from father to son.

Edward could not stop smiling as he held the knife in his hands.

"Thanks, Pa," he said, his voice filled with genuine gratitude.

He looked at the blade as if it were the most prized possession in the world, turning it over and over, marveling at its weight, the craftsmanship, and the sense of history that seemed to flow through it. For the rest of the journey, Edward kept the knife close, showing it off to anyone who would listen. It was as though the weight of his new responsibility had been made tangible in the form of that blade.

By the time they reached the outskirts of Bill's cabin, the journey had taken on a new pace. The landscape had begun to shift again, the forest thinning out as they neared the family's land. A familiar feeling of home washed over Woodrow as he spotted the small cabin in the distance. The air grew warmer, and the scent of wood smoke filled the breeze.

As they neared the cabin, the sound of a bloodhound's howl pierced the air. The dog's deep, booming cry echoed across the mountainside, a sound that had always been a part of their family's landscape. It rattled their bones with its intensity, and it made them both chuckle, remembering all the times they'd heard it growing up. The dog had a way of making its presence known, no matter where you were.

Bill, Woodrow's younger brother, appeared in the doorway, his face framed by a cloud of pipe smoke. His weathered hands cradled the clay pipe he had made himself, a small piece of craftsmanship that was part of his identity. When he saw Woodrow, his face lit up in recognition, and he strode toward them. Bill's gait was relaxed, as though time had slowed down just for them to reunite.

The moment they saw each other, they didn't just shake hands. Instead, they pulled each other into a bear hug, a hug filled with all the years of history, of shared experiences, of growing up together. Bill's laughter, rough and easy, echoed in the air as they clapped each other on the back. It was a greeting that only brothers could share—no need for words, just the bond of familiarity and love.

"Well now," Bill said, stepping back to look at his brothers. "What brings you men into our neck of the woods?" His voice was laced with curiosity, but also a touch of humor, as if he were already guessing what was to come.

Woodrow met his gaze, his eyes turning serious as he reached for the news he had been carrying all this time. "I've got some great news for you, little brother," he said, his voice soft but steady.

Inside the cabin, Elizabeth, Bill's wife, appeared with their children, and the atmosphere shifted to one of warmth and welcome. The cabin was humble, but it was filled with love, the kind of warmth only family could provide. The scent of coffee wafted from the hearth, making Edward's stomach growl in appreciation. But he remained outside, catching up with cousins he hadn't seen in what seemed like a year, since their maternal grandfather's passing. It was clear the cousins were glad to be reunited—there was laughter, shared memories, and a sense of joy that only family reunions could bring.

Inside, Woodrow's voice grew a little quieter as he continued. "The news I have to share is that the old cabin—the one Pa and his brothers built back in 28—is now yours."

Bill blinked in confusion, not quite grasping what his brother was saying. "What? You guys love that cabin. What happened, Woodrow?" His face was etched with a mixture of surprise and disbelief.

Woodrow met Bill's gaze, his expression softening. "We're moving, Bill. We're heading west—out to Indian Territory. The land out there is calling us, and we're going to settle there. It's time to start fresh, to make a new home for the family."

Bill was silent for a long moment, absorbing the weight of the news. His gaze flicked toward his children and his wife and then back to his brother. The decision was huge, and it left a lingering sense of melancholy in the air.

"Indian Territory," he repeated softly.

"That's a long way, Woodrow. What made you decide to go so far?"

Woodrow exhaled slowly, his shoulders heavy with the weight of his decision.

"It's time, Bill. We've got to move on, to grow and expand. This land has been good to us, but there's more out there for us. We need more space for the kids, for everything we're rebuilding."

Bill nodded slowly, understanding the weight of Woodrow's words. There was a sense of finality in the air, a recognition that this chapter of their lives was ending. But Bill also saw the determination in Woodrow's eyes, the same determination that had always been there. "Well," Bill said, his voice thick with emotion but laced with pride, "if it's what's best for your family, then I understand. You've always been the one to blaze the trail, little brother. I'm proud of you."

Woodrow smiled, his heart swelling with love and gratitude for his younger brother's understanding.

"I hope so, Bill. I really do."

Chapter 19
A Brother's Bond and A Final Promise

The morning was winding down, the sun now a little higher in the sky, casting long shadows that stretched across the yard. Woodrow stood beside his brother Bill, the air filled with the comforting smell of tobacco as they both prepared to enjoy a quiet moment before the long journey back home. Woodrow reached into his pocket, his large, weathered hands easily finding the familiar tobacco pouch. With a practiced motion, he pulled it out and opened the leather pouch, the scent of the tobacco mingling with the crisp mountain air. He had packed this pouch himself, the tobacco carefully chosen to suit his own tastes—flavored and rich, a taste that reminded him of long days spent working in the fields, sitting by the fire, and sharing stories with family.

Bill, standing just a little shorter than Woodrow, though still tall and lean, reached into his own pocket and pulled out his tobacco pouch with a smile. He held it out to his older brother, a silent offer that had become a ritual over the years. They traded pouches like they always did, exchanging an unspoken language of trust and familiarity. Bill preferred his tobacco a little sweeter, with a softer, milder flavor.

Woodrow liked his more robust and full-bodied. It was one of those small, personal touches that defined their bond. Even in the simplest moments, like this one, there was a deep connection—a reminder that no matter how far they went or how much time passed, they would always have these shared habits, these quiet moments to ground them.

As they packed their pipes, the ritual seemed to slow down time. The world around them was quiet, the sounds of the children in the cabin now distant as they eagerly awaited any news. Edward had already filled his cousins in on the family's big move, and Woodrow could tell by the glint in his son's eyes that the idea of moving into the old cabin was an exciting prospect for them. They were thrilled, especially at the thought of growing up in a place that held so many memories. The cabin, built so many years ago, would live on, but now it was time for a new generation to call it home.

As they finished preparing their pipes, Woodrow and Bill's gazes drifted back toward the open door of the cabin, where the children's heads could be seen peering out, their curiosity palpable. They were just children, still too young to fully understand the gravity of the move, but they were old enough to feel the excitement of a new adventure. The older ones, especially Edward, had already begun to tell them about the westward journey, about Indian Territory, about what lay ahead. The thought of starting over in a new land seemed to spark something in them—a hope for new beginnings, a chance to build something of their own.

Bill, who had always been the leaner and wirier of the two brothers, took a long stick from beside the table. He used it to lift the glass globe that covered the lantern, the warm light flickering beneath it. With a steady hand, he lit the stick, then used it to ignite Woodrow's pipe. The flame cast a warm glow on their faces, highlighting the years of weathered skin and the depth of their bond. Bill lit his own pipe next, his movements careful and deliberate, a small smile on his lips as the tobacco began to smoke, curling up into the air like the memories they were making together.

Woodrow sat back, taking a long draw from his pipe, savoring the moment before the inevitable farewell. Bill, who was always quick to speak what was on his mind, looked over at Woodrow and squinted slightly, his expression serious. There was something in his voice—a quiet understanding of how much had changed between them, how much was about to change.

"Big brother," Bill began, his voice rough from years of smoking and hard labor. I want to wish you good luck. I really appreciate your generosity in leaving the cabin to me." His tone was sincere, but there was an underlying sadness in his words. Woodrow was leaving behind more than just the cabin—it was a whole way of life, an entire chapter of their shared history.

Bill paused for a moment, his brows furrowing slightly as he looked at Woodrow, and then he added, "Brother, please just do me one favor. Promise me that when you get set up out there in the territory, you'll send word back to me. Let me know that you made it okay, and if you like what you find. Our family has been moving west for a while now, but we've never heard from them since they left. The only one who ever sent word was Uncle Byrd Lockhart, and he ended up founding his own town in Texas."

The words hit Woodrow harder than he had anticipated. He could feel the weight of his brother's request—Bill needed to know, needed to have some sign that their family was safe and thriving in the unknown territory they were about to enter. It was a promise that carried with it more than just words. It was about reassurance, about keeping the ties to home strong even when everything else seemed to be changing.

Woodrow's hand tightened around his pipe as he considered Bill's request. He exhaled a long stream of smoke into the quiet air, feeling the heaviness of the promise settle in his chest. "Brother, I promised you," Woodrow said, his voice firm, "Because we are going to make it. And I'll send word back to you, just like I promised. We'll make it work out there, and I'll make sure you hear from me."

With that, Woodrow stood up, the weight of his decision heavy on his shoulders. He knew the journey ahead would be long and difficult, but he had no doubt in his mind that he was doing what was best for his family. They were leaving behind everything they knew, but there was something about the challenge of the unknown that had always driven him.

Bill stood with him, his hand outstretched, and Woodrow shook it firmly. The grip was strong, both men holding onto it like a lifeline. But it wasn't just a handshake—it was a final promise between brothers, a bond that would survive even the miles and years between them. After shaking hands, they pulled each other into one last, powerful bear hug. It was a hug that spoke of everything they had been through together—childhood, family, hardship, love. It was a hug that could very well be the last time they embraced like this, at least for a long time.

Woodrow pulled back slowly, his voice softer now, carrying a sense of finality.

"One more week, brother," he said, his eyes catching Bill's.

"It'll all be yours. I even left Grandpa's rocking chair for you. I know it'll be in good hands."

Bill nodded, his eyes glistening with unshed emotion. He had always admired his older brother's strength, his ability to forge ahead, to make decisions, and to stand by them. But now, as he stood on the cusp of a new chapter, there was a sense of vulnerability in the air—a recognition that life would never quite be the same again.

As Woodrow turned and walked toward his son, holding the reins of the horses, the finality of their parting began to settle in. Bill stayed behind for a moment, watching them, then turned back toward the cabin, knowing that soon, the old place would be his, carrying with it the memories of their shared past. It was a bittersweet moment—a moment of love, loss, and hope all intertwined. The future was out there, in Indian Territory, and it was waiting for them.

Woodrow's goodbye and his promise to his brother

Chapter 20
A Race Against Time and the Elements

The rain had not stopped for three days, and each drop seemed like a symbol of the ever-growing urgency that weighed on Woodrow's shoulders. It had soaked into the earth, turning the ground into a soft, muddy mess that made every step a struggle. The cabin's roof groaned under the weight of the rain, and the persistent sound of water dripping from the eaves added to the quiet pressure that hung in the air.

Woodrow stood with Clara, his eyes scanning the smokehouse with a furrowed brow. The meat that hung inside was a lifeline—if it wasn't cured properly, it would spoil, leaving them without a crucial food source for the long journey ahead. Every minute felt like a race against time. The weather was a powerful force, one that didn't care about their plans or their need for efficiency. They were at its mercy.

Clara, as calm and collected as ever, knew how important it was to get the timing right. She had been helping Woodrow with the smokehouse for years, but never under conditions like these. The humidity from the rain made the smoke weak, causing the process to take longer than usual. She looked at the meat hanging, noting how the drying process was moving slowly, almost stubbornly.

"It'll take a few more days," she said, keeping her tone steady despite the mounting pressure.

"But we'll make it work. We always do."

Woodrow nodded, but the weight of the situation hung heavy on him. They couldn't afford any setbacks. The journey they were about to embark on required careful planning and preparation, and there was still so much left to do. He looked out through the smokehouse door, where David and Edward were working relentlessly to keep the fire going. The rain had made their work harder, but they were pushing through, chopping and splitting hickory wood to feed the fire.

Outside, the storm was unyielding, yet the boys continued their labor, knowing how essential it was to maintain the heat and smoke inside the smokehouse. The fire had to be kept at just the right temperature to cure the meat— too little heat, and it wouldn't last. Too much, and it would ruin the flavor and texture.

While the boys worked outside, Clara had taken charge of another important task: collecting eggs from the hens. It had been a week of constant collection, but Clara had managed to gather enough eggs to feed the family during the journey. Every day had been a race against the weather, and she had worked diligently to ensure nothing was wasted. It was a task she didn't mind—she'd grown accustomed to tending to the smaller details of their life, the quiet but essential responsibilities that kept everything running smoothly.

Tomorrow, she knew, would be a busy day. The smokehouse needed to be emptied and cleaned, and their belongings packed into the wagon. Woodrow had insisted on getting the rugged Chuckwagon for their journey—a vehicle that was both shelter and transport. Clara was grateful for the decision. With its many compartments and drawers, they would be able to pack their possessions securely. The wagon's thick canvas sides would protect them from the elements, offering some relief from the constant rain and the possibility of hail. It wasn't the ideal solution, but it was the best they could manage with the resources available.

But as much as the Chuckwagon was a blessing, it also posed a challenge. There simply wasn't enough room for everyone to sleep inside. The younger boys and the women would be sheltered in the wagon, but the older boys—and Woodrow himself—would have to sleep outside. They would have to make do, huddling under tarps or even just the open sky, with the knowledge that the weather would be unpredictable, and the wilderness unpredictable still.

Woodrow's mind wandered to the dangers that lay ahead. They had livestock tied around the wagon, and fresh meat would need to be guarded. He couldn't afford to let his guard down. Predators—wolves, coyotes, or even bears— were always lurking, waiting for a chance to take advantage of any weakness. His sons would need to be vigilant, watching the perimeter, and staying alert. They couldn't afford any mistakes.

As Woodrow pondered these dangers, Clara gave him a quiet, knowing look. She had seen the worry in his eyes, and while she shared his concerns, she had faith in their ability to make it work. They always did. "We'll make it work," he said, as much to reassure himself as to reassure her.

Clara didn't respond with words. Instead, she gave a small, reassuring smile, and that was enough. They had been through too much together to let anything, not even the worst of storms, break their resolve. They had survived the hardship of the smokehouse and the challenges of their land, and now they would survive the journey ahead.

Tomorrow, they would begin the final preparations—cleaning out the smokehouse, packing the wagon, and bracing for the unknown road ahead. It would be hard work, but they were used to it. There was no other choice. They would be leaving their old home behind, stepping into a new chapter in Indian Territory.

Woodrow couldn't help but feel the weight of the journey pressing down on him. He had done everything he could to prepare. He had planned every detail and considered every possibility. But there were always uncertainties. The road would be long and hard, and there would be challenges they couldn't foresee. But with his family by his side, he felt ready to face whatever came their way.

As the rain continued to fall outside, the family gathered around, the steady rhythm of their labor echoing through the cabin. Tomorrow would come, whether they were ready or not. But for now, they would make the most of the time they had, securing their future one step at a time.

Chapter 21
A New Beginning

Woodrow could hear the roosters crowing, their calls echoing through the hills like a chorus heralding the dawn of a new day. The sun had barely kissed the horizon, and already, the land around the cabin was coming to life. The day ahead would be one of great change. It would be the day that everything, every possession, and every memory, had to be packed into the wagon. The journey west awaited them, uncertain yet inevitable.

Clara had been up for an hour or so, her movements purposeful as she prepared breakfast with quiet determination. The aroma of sizzling bacon and freshly baked bread filled the small cabin, a comforting scent that clung to the air and wrapped around the family like a warm blanket. The sounds of the skillet and the crackle of firewood added to the symphony of early morning life in the cabin.

The kids had already taken care of their own responsibilities. Each of them had packed their belongings into their bags, and their clothes were neatly folded, waiting for the morning's rush. They had all known, for weeks now, that today would come, but now that it was here, there was an edge to the usual calm that had filled the homestead. Each one of them had a part to play in getting everything ready for the move, and they were all determined to make it happen.

Mary had been especially helpful to her ma, taking on the role of organizing the younger boys, making sure their things were packed properly, their clothes clean, and their minds focused. Woodrow watched her for a moment as she moved about with a quiet grace, the responsibility of the day settling on her shoulders. Mary had always been a steady hand in the household, but this move—this new life—was different. She could feel the weight of it in her bones, and yet, she didn't hesitate. She was the calm in the storm, the one who made sure that things ran smoothly.

Woodrow finished getting dressed, his worn boots creaking as he laced them up. The familiar feeling of the leather against his skin ground him in the moment. He could hear the boys stirring now, their voices a little groggy but filled with the energy of the day ahead. He knew it wouldn't be long before they'd be out of bed and ready to tackle the mountain of tasks that lay before them.

Before heading to the table, Woodrow made his way to the barn. The familiar smell of hay and the earthy scent of animals greeted him as he stepped inside. He made his way to the milking stall, where their Jersey cow stood patiently, waiting for him as she had every morning for the past few years. The cow had become a blessing to the family since the day they'd brought her home as a calf, the little creature that had nearly met her end at the hands of a grizzly bear. The boys had saved her then, working together to skin the bear and tend to the injured calf, an act that had bonded them to her in ways that words couldn't describe. RD had named her Lucky, and the name had stuck.

Woodrow smiled as he thought of that day, the memory clear as if it had just happened yesterday. The cow's survival was nothing short of miraculous, and she had become a symbol of hope and resilience for the family. She was going with them, as were all the animals. Each one had a story, a reason for making the journey with them. The Hereford bull, for example, had nearly died as a calf, but Mary had nursed him back to health, feeding him by hand until he was strong enough to graze on his own. She'd saved his life, and in turn, he had become an integral part of their lives.

When the milking was done, Woodrow took the full pail of fresh milk and made his way back to the cabin. He could feel the weight of the moment pressing down on him, the silence of the early morning broken only by the sounds of his boots crunching against the dirt. As he entered the cabin, the familiar warmth of the hearth wrapped around him, and the sight of his family gathered around the table brought a quiet sense of comfort.

The boys were already seated, each of them finding their favorite spots at the table, the same places they had sat for as long as Woodrow could remember. Clara was busy filling their cups with milk, her movements calm and practiced. She took the pail from him without a word, her hands working quickly as she served the boys their breakfast.

Woodrow looked around the table, his gaze lingering on each face, taking in the scene. The feeling that had settled in his gut, deep and unshakable, grew stronger. It was a feeling he hadn't had in years, not since the day his grandpa passed away five years ago. It was the same gnawing, uncertain feeling, the one that made his stomach churn and his thoughts race.

He knew exactly what was causing it. The question had been on his mind for weeks now: *Am I doing the right thing?* Was it right to pull his family away from everything they had ever known, to take them out west where nothing was certain? He had worked hard to build this life for them, but now he was asking them to leave it all behind. He wondered if it would be worth it if this move would truly bring them the happiness and security they sought. But those thoughts were fleeting, fading as quickly as they came. Woodrow had made up his mind. There was no turning back now.

He pushed the doubts aside, took a deep breath, and lowered his head along with the rest of his family. Clara's voice filled the room as she offered the morning prayer, her words a quiet blessing for the journey ahead. Woodrow joined in, his heart full of gratitude for what they had, even as his mind lingered on the uncertainties that lay ahead.

As the prayer ended, the family lifted their heads, and the feeling in Woodrow's gut seemed to soften, just a little. He knew that the road ahead wouldn't be easy, but he also knew that they would face it together, as they always had. They were more than just a family—they were a team. And with that, Woodrow stood, ready to face the day and whatever it would bring.

Chapter 22
The Final Preparations

Woodrow sat at the head of the table, his eyes sweeping over his family. The morning light filtered through the cabin's small windows, casting a soft glow on the faces of his children. He could see the quiet determination in each of them, the sense of purpose that had taken root in their hearts. They were ready, each of them playing their part in the journey ahead. He could feel the weight of the moment pressing down on him, the significance of what they were about to do. It wasn't just a journey—it was a new chapter in their lives.

The meal was finished. Plates were empty, and mugs were set down, a quiet hum of anticipation hanging in the air. Each one of them was looking at him now, waiting for his instructions. Woodrow's heart swelled with pride, but there was a knot in his stomach as well. The responsibility he carried was heavy, but he knew that this was the path they had to take.

"Alright, family," he said, his voice steady, "It's time."

His eyes met David's first. The boy was ready, a determined glint in his eye. "David and Edward, get the meat out of the smokehouse and hang it in its place in the wagon," Woodrow instructed. The boys nodded and moved quickly, heading toward the smokehouse, where the carefully cured meat was waiting to be packed away. Woodrow's gaze shifted to Ronald, then to Merle.

"Ronald, you and Merle get Red the bull tied to the tree next to the wagon. After everything and everyone is aboard, we'll tie him to the back of the wagon. The cows will follow him anywhere," he added.

Red had been a part of their lives for a long time, and Woodrow knew that the bull was the key to keeping the cattle in line. His steady presence would ensure the journey went smoothly.

"RD," Woodrow continued, his tone calm but firm, "Take your brother Paul and ride down the hill to the neighbors. Tell Miss Annie they can come get the chickens in the morning. We'll lock them in the coop before we leave."

The chickens, too, had a place in this transition, and Woodrow trusted RD and Paul to take care of that detail.

"We have four mares, one gelding, and a stud," Woodrow went on, his eyes moving over the boys. "David and Edward will drive behind us when we leave. The only ones riding horses are myself, David, Edward, and Merle."

It was clear that everyone had a role, a task to complete. The excitement of the journey was building, but so was the realization that it wasn't just a new beginning—it was a farewell. The land they were leaving behind had shaped them and had witnessed their triumphs and struggles. But now, they were moving forward, and Woodrow could feel the weight of the unknown ahead.

Clara and Mary made their final trip to the cabin. Woodrow could see them working together, lifting crates, organizing what little was left to pack. The cabin was nearly empty now, the belongings that had once filled every nook and cranny were now stowed away, ready for the long journey. They had worked together as a family, each person contributing in their own way.

"There's one more thing to do," Woodrow said, his voice cutting through the quiet. "And it's one of the most important things we need to do before we go."

The boys turned their attention to him. Woodrow's eyes settled on each of them, his voice lowering as he gave his next instruction. "Boys, get your new rifles out and get 'em loaded up for target practice."

He paused, letting the words sink in.

"Edward, grab that big log of firewood and prop it up on that oak tree next to the barn. It's about a hundred and fifty feet away and should make a good target."

The boys sprang into action, the excitement of shooting filling the air. Woodrow had always believed in teaching them to be precise, to be sure of themselves in every aspect of their lives. This rifle, the one they had just acquired, would make all the difference on this journey. It would be their protector, their tool for survival in the wild, and he wanted to make sure each of them could wield it with confidence.

David was first. He stood tall, his rifle steady in his hands. He aimed the log and pulled the trigger. The shot rang out, echoing across the valley, and the log splintered down the center, falling to the ground with a satisfying thud. David looked at his father, a grin spreading across his face. "This is enough," he said, his voice filled with pride.

They walked over to the log to inspect the damage. The split was clean and precise. Woodrow nodded, impressed. "I guess one shot was enough," he said, his voice gruff with approval.

Edward, eager to show his skills, took his turn. He aimed carefully and fired. The log split down the middle just as David's had. Edward's face lit up with excitement. "This rifle is the best gun ever made," he said, his voice full of admiration.

Ronald, not wanting to be outdone by his brothers, took his shot next. Like them, his aim was true. The log split cleanly in two, and Ronald's grin mirrored Edward's. The rifle's power was undeniable.

Woodrow stepped forward, his turn now. "David, put two logs together for me to shoot," he instructed. David and Edward worked quickly, placing the logs in position. Woodrow aimed, steadying his breath. He squeezed the trigger, and the shot rang out, powerful and sharp. The logs exploded, splitting with ease. Woodrow lowered his rifle and looked at his sons, a sense of satisfaction washing over him. "This rifle will make the difference on this trip," he said, his voice resolute.

The family gathered around, each of them feeling the weight of the moment. They had practiced their aim, and now they were ready.

"Okay, family, we're off to our first town," Woodrow said, the words slipping from his lips like a promise. "Knoxville."

The wagon was packed, the animals ready, and the rifles loaded. The sun was climbing higher in the sky, the day unfolding before them like a road they could not yet see. The journey west awaited, full of uncertainty and promise. But as Woodrow looked around at his family, he knew that no matter what lay ahead, they would face it together. The road was theirs to travel, and with their strength and unity, there was nothing they couldn't overcome.

Chapter 23
The Journey Begins

The day had unfolded as they set out from their home, the wagon rolling steadily over the uneven terrain. The rugged path was tough, with rocks jutting out and ditches carved deep into the earth, but the wagon handled it with ease. Woodrow, guiding the team with a firm but gentle hand, could feel the rhythm of the journey taking hold. It was a long road ahead, but the wagon was sturdy and dependable, just like the family riding in it. He glanced back at the boys, each one of them busy at their task, as he had directed.

Ronald had come a long way since the early days, and today, he had proven himself a capable wagon hand. He was steady with the reins, his movements confident as he maneuvered the wagon through the rocky stretches. Woodrow had always believed that the best way to teach his sons was to give them responsibility, and Ronald had risen to the challenge. He could see it in the way he held the reins, in the way he kept his eyes sharp, scanning the path ahead.

David, ever vigilant, tied a lead rope to the stud to keep the horse from wandering too far. This task required patience, and Woodrow knew David had the temperament for it. The stud was a fine animal, strong and independent, but he had a tendency to stray. David was always quick to rein him in, keeping him close to the wagon.

Read the bull, as steady as ever, followed along behind the wagon with the cows trailing in tow. Woodrow couldn't help but feel a deep sense of gratitude for the animals that had been with them through thick and thin. They had a story of their own, each one carrying its own history, its own place in this journey. Red, the bull, was as much a part of this family as the boys themselves.

It would take them about three days to reach Knoxville, and the military path they followed was well-worn and easy to navigate. The soldiers who had traveled this route before had laid the groundwork, and the big creeks were bridged with massive timbers, strong enough to carry their heavy loads across. The road was marked by history, and Woodrow couldn't help but appreciate the ingenuity of those who had come before them. Every bridge, every turn, was a reminder that they were walking in the footsteps of others, treading a path that had been carved through struggle and survival.

As the sun began to dip toward the horizon, casting a warm, golden hue across the landscape, Woodrow knew it wouldn't be long before nightfall. The shadows grew longer, and the air cooled, signaling that the day was coming to an end. He motioned to Ronald, signaling for him to follow as they began to look for a place to set up camp for the night.

Ahead, a clearing appeared, bathed in the soft light of the setting sun. It was perfect—a place where they could rest and let the animals graze. The grass was lush, and the animals would have plenty to feed on before being tied up for the night. But Woodrow didn't take any chances. He liked to keep their camp a few hundred yards away from the road, just in case any strangers happened to wander by in the dark. He preferred to keep their presence low, hidden in the woods if necessary. The cover provided by the trees would offer a retreat in case of danger, and it also kept the animals safe from being spotted too easily.

Ronald guided the wagon into the clearing, pulling up the brakes with a practiced hand. The camp was soon set up, and the family sprang into action. Clara and Mary, as always, were quick to take charge of the preparations. The fire crackled to life, sending a warm glow into the surrounding darkness. The sound of pans clanging and food being stirred in the wagon filled the air. There was something comforting about the rhythm of their tasks, the way they all knew exactly what needed to be done.

David and Edward had finished tending to the animals and entered the camp, their faces tired but satisfied. Woodrow could see the weariness in their eyes, but also the pride. They were doing something important, something they could all be proud of.

With the younger boys, Woodrow moved to the wagon and began attaching the canvas to the side, creating a roof to shield them from the elements. It was a simple task, but it had to be done right. They worked together, pulling and securing the canvas with practiced hands, creating a shelter for the night.

Soon, the smell of food began to fill the air. The women had prepared a hearty meal—slab smoked ham, brown beans, and cornbread. The aroma was rich, comforting, and familiar. For a moment, it felt almost like home, like the life they had known before the journey began. The only difference was the vast sky above them, the stars beginning to twinkle as night settled in. Woodrow looked up at the heavens, feeling a sense of peace wash over him. In that moment, he knew that they were being watched over, that God's hand was guiding them on this path.

As the family gathered around the fire, sharing the meal, there was a quiet sense of unity. They had come together for this moment, this journey, and though the road ahead was uncertain, they knew they would face it together. The challenges of the day were behind them, and tomorrow would bring new obstacles and new tasks. But for now, they were together, and that was enough.

As the night deepened, Woodrow sat back, content. The fire crackled, the stars shimmered above, and the sounds of the wilderness surrounded them. They were on their way. They had made it this far, and no matter what lay ahead, they would face it as a family. This journey was just beginning, but they were ready.

It begins heading westward

Chapter 24
An Unexpected Visit

The early morning air was still crisp when the sound of the two Walker hounds stirred everyone from their sleep. The dogs were known for their keen senses, and their barking was a familiar wake-up call. Woodrow had the first watch last night, and the stillness of the wilderness had passed without incident. Now, David had taken the second watch, and he was up early, scanning the horizon as he checked on the dogs. His eyes narrowed as he observed two riders approaching in the distance.

"Pa, there's a couple of riders heading this way," David called out, his voice steady but alert.

Woodrow, already dressed and on his feet, reached for his new rifle, his fingers tightening around its smooth wooden stock. He didn't want to take any chances. The rifle felt like a part of him now—a tool of protection, a promise to keep his family safe.

"Son, get your rifle and get it ready. Tell your brothers to do the same," Woodrow instructed, his voice low but commanding.

The family stirred as David relayed the message to his brothers, each of them making their way to their respective spots, rifles in hand. They knew what to do—watch, wait, and be prepared. It was a skill learned out of necessity, the knowledge that danger could come from anywhere in the wilderness. Woodrow's eyes stayed fixed on the approaching riders, his mind running through possible scenarios. He knew they had to be cautious, but there was also a sense of something familiar about the situation.

As the riders drew nearer, the landscape cleared just enough for Woodrow to make out the figures more clearly. His breath caught in his chest as recognition struck him. The riders were Jack, an old friend from years past, and his son Andrew.

"Jack? Is that you?" Woodrow called out, a smile tugging at his lips as he lowered his rifle. The tension that had built up in his chest loosened as he recognized his friend's familiar face.

Jack's voice rang out in return, rough with age and dust, but unmistakable. "I thought that was your hounds, my friend. You never forget that sound, do you? We've run plenty of coons up a tree together, haven't we?"

Woodrow chuckled, the memories flooding back. There had been many nights, long and cold, spent hunting with Jack. The camaraderie of those times, the crackling fire, the thrill of the chase—it felt like a lifetime ago, but it was a bond that hadn't dulled over the years.

"Jack, it's good to see you," Woodrow said, motioning for the riders to come closer.

"Hop down, have some breakfast with us. It's been too long."

Jack shook his head, a smile on his weathered face, though his eyes held a certain urgency.

"We'd love to, Woodrow, but we're headed to Knoxville. Just need a bit of coffee before we hit the trail again."

"Well, I reckon we'll be heading there too," Woodrow replied, gesturing toward his family, who were now gathering around the campfire. "You might as well eat a good breakfast and tag along with us for a while."

Jack's brow furrowed as he looked at Woodrow, a touch of concern creeping into his voice.

"What's going on here, my friend? I heard a little about you all moving out west, but I didn't think it was true. Thought it was just talk."

Woodrow met Jack's gaze, his expression was solemn but resolute.

"It's all true, Jack. We're headed west. You might as well eat up and travel with us to Knoxville. There's no sense in rushing off when we could use the company."

Jack hesitated for a moment, glancing at Andrew, who was already tending to the horses.

"Coffee sounds good," he said with a nod. "But we need to get there and back home quickly. My wife's brother and his kids are moving to our mountain, so we need to show them the way."

Woodrow understood the urgency in his old friend's voice. Time was precious, and the road they all traveled was long and uncertain. After Jack finished his coffee, they exchanged a few more words, reminiscing about old times, before Jack stood up, his boots crunching on the dirt as he prepared to leave.

"See ya again someday, buddy," Jack called out, clapping Woodrow on the back.

"Take care, Jack," Woodrow replied, his voice filled with the weight of a promise that neither of them could quite put into words.

As the two riders turned their horses and rode off into the distance, Woodrow watched them go. For a moment, the world felt smaller, as if the vast expanse of the wilderness had drawn together just enough for old friends to meet, even if only for a brief time. But the road ahead was calling, and there was no time to linger.

Woodrow turned back to his family, his heart filled with the familiar sense of purpose that had driven him all these years. He looked around at his sons and daughter, all of them ready and waiting. "Well, we better get it going," he said, his voice steady and firm.

The family gathered around the fire for a quick breakfast. There was a sense of calm now, the early morning bustle giving way to the familiar routine of the journey. Clara and Mary worked together to serve the meal, while the boys packed up their things, ready to continue the trek.

Once the last crumbs were eaten and the campfire was doused, the family packed their gear onto the wagon. The horses were hitched, the animals readied, and the wagon was set to roll once more. Woodrow gave one last look at the spot where Jack and Andrew had ridden off, then turned to his family with a nod.

"Let's hit the trail, folks," he said, his voice filled with quiet determination.

The path ahead was still long, the uncertainty of the journey never far from their minds. But for now, they had the strength of each other, and that was enough to keep them going.

Baby Beaver Story

Chapter 25
The Baby Beaver

It had been three long days, and the familiar outline of Knoxville finally appeared on the horizon, twinkling like a beacon against the setting sun. The fading light of day cast a soft glow over the landscape, signaling that they were almost there. Woodrow, with his keen sense of time, knew they needed to make camp soon.

"Let's make camp, boys," he called out to his sons, his voice carrying the authority of years of guiding his family through long journeys.

He paused for a moment, taking in the landscape, before speaking again, his tone more serious.

"Now, we're close to a big town, and there'll be a lot of folks coming and going, so let's be vigilant tonight. We don't know who we'll run into."

The camp was quickly set up, each of them knowing their tasks and working together with practiced ease. Clara and Mary had been hard at work earlier, and now the camp was filled with the delicious smell of supper. Chicken and dumplings—one of Woodrow's favorite meals. Clara had opened up a few of her jars of boiled chicken, and the rich, savory smell made everyone's stomachs growl in anticipation.

Once the meal was served and everyone had settled down, the boys relaxed around the fire. Woodrow leaned back, taking out his old pipe, and with a deep puff of smoke, he let the familiar feeling of the evening calm his mind. As the warmth of the fire flickered in his eyes, little Allen, his youngest, hopped onto his lap with a bright smile, his face eager for attention.

"Pa, would you tell us a story, please?" Allen asked, his voice filled with excitement. The other boys nodded enthusiastically, their faces hopeful, knowing their father's stories were always the highlight of their evenings.

Woodrow smiled at his youngest, setting his pipe aside.

"Alright, alright," he said, his voice warm and inviting as he shifted his posture and looked down at Allen.

"Have I ever told you the story about me and my best friend Marvin catching a baby beaver?"

The moment the words left his mouth, he could see the attention on their faces sharpen. All of his boys were leaning in, eager to hear, their eyes wide in expectation. Little Allen, nestled in his lap, practically beamed with joy, while the older boys sat just as close, listening intently.

"Well, it all started one evening, almost dark. Marvin and I were twelve years old, camping down by the riverbank," Woodrow began, his voice taking on the nostalgic tone of one reliving a cherished memory. "We'd been catching catfish all day, and we had a fire going, ready to eat our last fish."

He paused for a moment, taking in the firelight flickering in their faces before continuing.

"All of a sudden, Marvin pointed towards something swimming towards us. "What's that?" he asked, squinting into the water. "It must be a snake or a fish!" We watched for a few minutes, and then the head of whatever it was finally poked through the water. And I'll be damned, it wasn't a snake, it wasn't a fish—it was a baby beaver."

A chorus of "No way!" and "Really?" broke out from the boys, and Woodrow chuckled at their amazement.

"It just sat there for a minute, looking at us, then shook off the water like a little dog," he continued, smiling at the memory. "Marvin looked at me like, Do you believe this?" Then, Marvin, being Marvin, started making sounds like a baby puppy. "And what do you know? The baby beaver started waddling up the bank toward us."

The boys were hanging on every word now, eyes wide in disbelief, as they envisioned the unlikely scene unfolding.

"Now that's unbelievable, right?" Woodrow went on. "But it didn't stop there. It came right up to Marvin and stopped, just close enough to be picked up. It wasn't trying to escape or anything. It just sat there, right in Marvin's arms. We started petting it like it was a puppy, and it never moved. We kept it warm next to the fire all night."

Woodrow's voice softened with a sense of reverence. "We forgot all about our catfish on the stringer in the water. We weren't even hungry anymore. Petting a real baby beaver—it was the most amazing thing I'd ever seen."

The boys exchanged astonished looks, their minds unable to fathom the miracle their father was describing.

"Who's ever done this before, right?" Woodrow continued.

"It was a blessing, something that only God himself could've directed, sending that little creature to us. Normally, we're the hunters, not the ones being befriended by the animals."

The boys were nearly breathless with excitement, but the questions came quickly. "Pa, what happened to it? What did you do with it?"

Woodrow looked at his sons, his face calm but filled with the wisdom of someone who had seen much.

"Well, we figured it had to be hungry, so when the sun came up, we put it back in the water. It swam off and disappeared, and we never saw it again."

The boys sat in quiet wonder, each of them reflecting on the story in their own way. Woodrow smiled as he patted Allen's head and stood up, stretching his legs.

"Alright, let's get to bed, my family," he said with a yawn. "Tomorrow will be another story in itself."

With a shared sense of warmth from the fire and the comfort of each other's company, the family settled down for the night. Tomorrow, they would continue their journey toward Knoxville, but for now, they had their stories to carry them through. And in the stillness of the night, as the stars began to shine above them, Woodrow couldn't help but feel grateful for the simple, miraculous moments that made their journey so special.

Chapter 26
A Stop in Knoxville

The morning air was brisk as Woodrow and his family made their way into Knoxville. The hustle and bustle of the town reminded Woodrow of a chicken yard, with everyone running around without a clear direction. He kept a sharp eye on the busy streets, narrowly avoiding a collision with a passing wagon.

"Let's stop by the blacksmith, boys," Woodrow called to his sons, squinting as he looked for the shop. One of the back wheels on their wagon had a few loose spokes that needed tightening up, and it was better to get it fixed now than wait until they were out on the trail again.

The town was lively, full of the typical clamor of people rushing about, but it wasn't long before Woodrow spotted the blacksmith shop on the edge of town. He motioned to Ronald to follow him, guiding the wagon toward the shop. What a sight they must have made—an entire family, a wagon, animals, and riders leading and following in a long procession through the town. They surely looked out of place among the more modern folk of Knoxville.

Pulling to a stop in front of the shop, Woodrow set the brake. Clara, Mary, and the younger boys jumped out of the wagon, stretching their arms and legs to get the blood flowing after the long ride.

"Alright, boys, water the animals and stick around here while I take care of the wagon," Woodrow instructed, before making his way toward the blacksmith's office.

As he approached, a man emerged from the side of the shop. Before Woodrow could speak, the man greeted him with a friendly tone.

"Can I help ya, sir?"

"Yes, sir, you can. I just bought this wagon about a week ago, and we've come all the way from Jonesborough," Woodrow explained, gesturing to the back wheel.

"Some of the spokes on the right rear wheel are loose and need tightening."

"Ah, no problem at all, sir," the blacksmith replied with a smile. "We'll have that fixed up in no time."

Woodrow extended his large, calloused hand for a handshake.

"Woodrow Lockhart," he said, nodding with a firm shake.

"William Dillan," the blacksmith replied, returning the nod.

"That's quite the rig you have there, sir. Where ya headed?"

Woodrow shifted his weight, his boots crunching on the gravel as he answered.

"We're heading west, to the Indian Territory."

"Well, you've got quite a bit of ground to cover then," William remarked, raising an eyebrow. "But I reckon you've got it under control."

Woodrow smiled slightly. "Yes, sir. Could you point me to the general store? We need to pick up a few supplies and some fresh water."

"Sure thing," William said, gesturing down the street.

"The general store is just a few hundred yards down on the left. You can't miss it—there's a big sign that says 'Wilson Marketplace.' As for water, I've got a good well behind the shop. You're welcome to fill up your barrels, no charge."

Woodrow nodded, grateful for the help. He turned back toward Clara and the boys, giving them directions. "The store is down the street on the left. If you want to pick up a few supplies or maybe a piece of hard candy for the boys, it's fine. Here," he said, handing Clara a few gold coins. "Get whatever you need, darling. I'll be here for a little while."

Woodrow turned back to William. "Thanks again for the help. If you don't mind, we'll move the wagon to the well in the back so the boys can fill up the water barrels while you tighten up the spokes."

"No problem, sir," William said with a wave.

"I'll take care of the wheel while you get the water."

Ronald gave his father a nod and headed toward the well with David following close behind. Edward, Clara, and the younger boys made their way to the marketplace, eager to see what the store had to offer.

Woodrow led his horse around back, where he watered it at the trough. For now, the animals were securely housed in a pen at the blacksmith shop, and they were getting plenty of feed and water while they waited for the wagon to be repaired.

Before long, they'd be back on the road, heading toward the next town on their journey.

Chapter 27
The Wheel Repair and A Sweet Surprise

Mr. Dillan finished his work on the wagon wheel and approached Woodrow, wiping his hands on a rag. "All done with the wheel," he said.

"I checked all your wheels and greased them up good. I'll add a tub of new grease to the bill. And I recommend keeping a close eye on your wheels, especially when you're crossing rocks or going through water. Check 'em every morning before you head out."

Woodrow nodded thoughtfully.

"Thanks for the advice. I'll make sure to keep an eye on everything."

He then called to his boys.

"Ronald, David, go ahead and hook up the team to the wagon. The animals need to come out of the pen, too."

As the boys worked to prepare the wagon, David noticed their family coming down the street. He motioned to Ronald and pointed excitedly.

"Pa, there they are!"

Woodrow finished his conversation with Mr. Dillan, shaking his hand gratefully.

"Thanks again, my friend. We'll definitely keep an eye on the wheels and axles."

Clara and the rest of the family were approaching, each of them carrying a sack of supplies. Even little Allen had a sack slung over his shoulder. He was grinning from ear to ear, clearly pleased with whatever treasure he had inside.

Woodrow couldn't resist and scooped up his youngest son into his arms. "Son, do you have something special in that sack for me?"

Allen nodded eagerly, a big smile lighting up his face. "Yep, Pa!"

Woodrow chuckled. "Let's take a peek then."

Allen eagerly dug into his sack and pulled out a handful of hard candy.

"Boy, howdy, son, you've got enough candy here to feed the whole town!" Woodrow said in amazement.

Allen giggled and reached into his sack again, pulling out another piece of candy.

"Here, Pa, this is for you!"

Woodrow opened his mouth as Allen carefully placed the peppermint candy inside. Woodrow smiled, savoring the sweetness. "Goodness, would you look at that... peppermint, my favorite kind!" he said, his heart full of joy at the simple gesture.

After a moment, Woodrow set Allen back down and helped him climb into the wagon. Turning to the rest of the family, he called, "Alright, let's get loaded up. We've got a long journey ahead of us."

With the wagon packed and the animals ready, the family prepared to continue their journey, feeling grateful for the small pleasures and the kindness of strangers along the way.

Chapter 28
The Long Ride West

Woodrow mounted his horse with a quiet determination, his eyes scanning the wagon, the stock, and the familiar faces that had come to rely on his every move. The sun hung low behind him, casting long golden shadows over the rugged trail ahead. He turned to the group, his voice steady, laced with grit and calm resolve.

"It'll probably take every bit of a week to get to Cookeville," he said, nodding toward the trail that curled like a ribbon through the hills.

Everything seemed in place. The wagon creaked with supplies, horses snorted in the cool breeze, and the others—Ronald, David, Clara, Mary, and the boys—were ready. They were more than just travelers now. They were a family in motion, a caravan of hope inching westward toward promise, uncertainty, and all that lay in between.

The blacksmith back in town had warned him of the journey: creeks swollen from spring rains, hills so steep they might force even the military to turn back. But he had also said, "Stick to the main trail, you'll make it fine." Woodrow had taken that advice to heart. The land ahead was a challenge, but so was everything they'd already endured.

The first day passed without incident. The wagon rolled smoothly over the packed dirt trail, and the horses responded well. But Woodrow knew better than to grow comfortable. This was just the beginning. The real test would come in the days ahead—steep ascents, muddy fords, axle-breaking ruts. He had calculated five weeks to reach the edge of Indian Territory. Fort Smith, Arkansas, was the mark, and even that was just a doorway to the vast unknown beyond. Others had made it, scarred but standing. If they had no major breakdowns, they might just do the same.

As dusk fell, brushing the hills with lavender and burnt orange, Woodrow signaled to Ronald with a silent wave. They veered off the main trail into a small clearing flanked by sycamores and sweetgum trees. The air smelled of earth and honeysuckle, the ground dry and firm—good enough for camp.

The wagon groaned to a halt. The animals were tended to—fed, watered, and calmed. The boys unstrapped their saddles, setting them beside the wagon. Their new rifles gleamed faintly in the fading light, propped within easy reach, a quiet reminder of the dangers that might lurk just beyond the firelight.

Clara and Mary had been busy, and when supper was served, it nearly brought tears to Woodrow's eyes. There, in the middle of nowhere, under an open sky, they sat down to a meal that tasted like home. Thick, tender beefsteak seared to perfection. Potatoes fried with slivers of onion, the smell alone enough to stir memories of his mother's kitchen. And fresh, crusty bread still warm from the pan.

"Well now," Woodrow said, his voice rough with emotion. "Clara, Mary… you two could cook the finest meal anywhere, anytime."

Clara chuckled, brushing a strand of hair from her brow. "Thank you, Woodrow. We had a little help from the town. Picked up the steaks at the marketplace. And for dessert— apple pie."

A quiet murmur of appreciation rose from the group as she uncovered the pie, its golden crust glistening, the scent of cinnamon wrapping around it like a blanket.

"Enjoy, everyone," Clara said with a warm smile.

Woodrow turned his eyes toward David, his eldest. "Son," he said, his voice low and respectful, "Would you do the honor of saying grace?"

David looked stunned for a heartbeat. His father had never asked him before. This was more than a meal—it was a passing of the torch. He nodded solemnly, then lowered his head, his voice steady though his hands trembled slightly.

"Lord," he began, "We thank You for keeping us safe on the trail, for the health of our family, and for the food You've provided. We know the road ahead is long, but we trust you'll walk it with us. And thank You, Lord… for the parents You've blessed us with. They give us strength, love, and light."

He paused, just for a breath, then finished: "Amen."

A hush followed the prayer, heavy with meaning. The fire crackled. The horses shifted. And at that moment, under the open sky, they were more than travelers.

They were blessed.

Chapter 29
Trouble on the Trail

The trail ahead was no friend to the weary. For two days straight, the wagon groaned like a tired old man with each bump and jolt along the uneven military road. If it could still be called that. Time and weather had ravaged it — the rains carved gullies deep enough to swallow a wheel whole, and jagged rocks lay scattered like bones. Hills rose and fell like waves, and the valleys, once gentle and green, were now cut with scars of old floods.

It wasn't just the land that seemed worn; even the air felt tired, weighed down by the long stretch of travel and the uncertainty ahead. But they pressed on.

Woodrow rode at the head, every nerve alert. His eyes scanned the path, his ears tuned to the creak of leather, the rhythmic clatter of hooves, and the occasional distant call of a hawk overhead. His hands were slick from axle grease — Mr. Dillan, back in the last town, had given him more than enough, but they were already going through it faster than expected. Without it, the wheels would seize, the axles would burn out, and the wagon, their only shelter and carrier of provisions, would be dead weight.

Clara leaned out of the wagon and gave him a small wave.

"We've still got enough supplies," she called. "Don't see a need to stop in Cookeville unless we're needing something urgent."

Woodrow nodded thoughtfully.

"We'll stop by the blacksmith. Pick up more grease if he's got any to spare. I got a feelin' this road's gonna keep eatin' what we've got."

He crouched to check the wheels. The wooden spokes were tight. For now. One less worry.

That afternoon, the trail began its descent toward a winding creek nestled in a narrow valley. The road dipped low, and Woodrow, riding ahead, pulled his horse to a halt. He studied the path carefully — there, in the bend, the water slowed, meandering through the brush like a silver ribbon. It was the best crossing he'd seen all day. But one problem remained — a downed tree blocked the trail, its thick trunk half-buried in the soil, branches fanned out like a challenge to their journey.

Woodrow turned in the saddle and waved a hand.

David and Merle were already climbing from their horses, axes in hand. They didn't wait for orders. They knew their father's signal, and they knew their place. The boys had grown into men on this road — sweat, blisters, and the rhythm of responsibility had forged them into more than just passengers. They were protectors of the family now.

Their blades bit into the bark with clean, purposeful strikes. Woodrow watched for a moment, pride quietly warming his chest. He had raised them right. Hardworking. Fearless. Faithful.

But something shifted in the air.

It was the horses — they knew it first. One of the mares reared slightly, eyes wide and nostrils flaring. Then another stamped its hooves anxiously.

David paused, axe raised. He scanned the treeline. His heartbeat quickened.

There, a dark shape emerged from the woods. A massive grizzly bear, at least three hundred yards away, moving with that slow, terrifying grace that only predators possessed. Its coat was matted with mud, its breath steaming in the cooling air. It was watching them.

David didn't speak — he just turned to Merle. Their eyes met, and that was enough.

"Rope," David said, voice low and steady.

Merle swung it off his saddle and tossed it across the trail. David caught it in one motion, wrapped it around the base of the tree, and pulled it tight.

"Mount up," he ordered.

"We drag it clear. Quick and clean."

Both brothers swung into their saddles. They backed their horses until the rope stretched taut, then, with a unified command, spurred them forward. The tree groaned against the earth's grip, roots crackling, soil tearing. Slowly, stubbornly, it shifted. Just enough.

Once the path was clear, David dismounted and coiled the rope back onto his saddle. His eyes swept the treeline again.

The bear was gone.

The woods were silent, as if nothing had ever happened — as if the wilderness had simply decided to let them go.

But everyone knew better. Out here, the land gave nothing for free.

"We best get back," David said quietly.

"Before he changes his mind."

They rode hard back to the wagon, dusk now falling around them like a curtain. The air had cooled, and the campfire would soon be needed. As they returned, Clara looked up from where she'd been sorting supplies and gave them a questioning glance.

Woodrow just gave a quiet nod. No words were needed. Not tonight.

The trail west was full of unknowns — wild creatures, rough terrain, sudden storms — but more than any of that, it was full of tests. Of patience. Of courage. Of heart.

And tonight, the road had tested them again.

And once more, the family had answered.

Chapter 30
The Grizzly Story

The sun had just dipped behind the hills, casting long golden shadows across the valley, when David and Merle rejoined the wagon party. The air smelled of dust and pine sap, the distant murmur of the creek still audible in the hush between hoofbeats.

Woodrow was standing near the wagon tongue, arms crossed, a sharp eye on the trail ahead. When he saw his sons returning, he raised a hand in greeting, relief flickering in his chest. They were safe, but they were late.

"You get that tree moved?" he called out, half-expecting a shrug and a nod.

David opened his mouth to respond, but before a single word could escape, he felt a tug at his sleeve. He looked down to see Merle, eyes alight with mischief and adrenaline, leaning close.

"Let me tell it, Dave," Merle whispered.

"Please. Don't tell Pa. I wanna be the one."

David looked at his younger brother, noting the faint tremble of excitement in his voice and the way his chest puffed up with pride. He smiled and gave him a playful nudge.

"Go on, then. Tell him."

Merle didn't need to be told twice.

He edged closer to their father, so close he could almost grab his arm if he needed reassurance, though he wouldn't admit it. His voice started soft, but his eyes were wide, animated by what he'd just lived through.

"Pa," he began, drawing the word out, "Just as we were finishin' up choppin' that tree, the horses started gettin' real spooked. I mean ears-back, eyes-rollin", stompin'-their-hooves kinda spooked."

Woodrow cocked a brow, trying not to smile.

"We stopped swingin' the axes and looked up," Merle continued, his voice rising with every word.

"And Pa — you ain't gonna believe what we saw."

Woodrow leaned in a little, folding his arms tighter. "I don't know, son. What'd you see?"

Merle inhaled dramatically, chest puffed. "It was the biggest, meanest-looking grizzly bear I've ever seen in my life! And it wasn't far either — maybe three hundred yards, just starin' at us like we were dinner."

Woodrow's mouth twitched with the beginnings of a grin, but he kept quiet, letting Merle have his moment.

"David looked at me and yelled to grab his rope. I threw it over, and he tied it to the tree like lightning. Told me to hook my end to my saddle, and he did the same. We didn't have time to think — just pulled that tree right outta the way like we'd done it a hundred times."

Merle paused for effect, his voice lowering to a dramatic hush. "We dragged it just far enough for the wagon to pass through, then we got outta there fast. I swear, Pa, I just knew we were goners."

By now, Woodrow's laughter was pressing at the edges of his composure, but he just nodded, his voice warm with pride. "Well now… that's one mighty fine tale, son. You both kept your heads and did what needed doin'. That's what matters."

Merle beamed, his chest lifting just a little higher.

"But," Woodrow added, glancing toward the darkening woods, "looks like we'll be passin' through that ol' bear's territory. Best hope he lets us through without much fuss."

The conversation shifted into quiet as the night deepened around them. The sky turned from bruised purple to deep black, stars beginning to prick through the fabric of the heavens. The fire crackled softly, casting flickering light over the wagon wheels and the tired faces of the family.

Woodrow volunteered for the first watch. He sat by the fire with his rifle laid across his lap, his ears tuned for every snap of a twig or rustle of a brush. He wasn't about to rest easy with a full-grown grizzly possibly still roaming nearby.

Around two in the morning, he walked over to the wagon and nudged David gently awake.

"Your turn, son," he whispered.

"Keep a sharp eye, especially on the animals. If that bear's hungry, they'll be his first target."

David rubbed the sleep from his eyes and nodded, rising quietly. Woodrow tossed another few logs on the fire, sending up a flurry of sparks. The flames climbed higher, casting a protective glow over the camp.

He gave one last look toward the tree line before settling into a light doze. His thoughts drifted to his sons — how they'd worked together, faced danger without flinching, and protected the family without being told.

Out here on the trail, every day brought a new challenge, a new test. And tonight, the test had come in the form of a grizzly.

But what mattered most wasn't the size of the danger. It was the strength of those who stood against it, and the bond between them that refused to break.

Chapter 31
Through Cookeville

The first pale rays of morning light filtered through the trees, casting a soft glow over the campsite. A breeze stirred the ashes in the fire pit and whispered through the tall grass beyond the wagons.

Woodrow and David were already up, the fire stoked back to life, and the smell of boiling coffee drifting lazily into the air. The night had passed in peace, and the grizzly, perhaps sensing the watchful eyes and loaded rifles, had chosen discretion over boldness.

David handed out tin cups, steam curling from each one. When Woodrow offered Clara her cup, she took it with both hands and a small, knowing smile.

"Thank you," she said, adding a playful wink that made Woodrow chuckle softly before turning back to the fire.

Soon, the rest of the camp was awake — boots thudding on dirt, yawns stretching into low conversation, and the sizzle of breakfast on the skillet adding music to the morning. By the time the sun had cleared the ridge, everyone was dressed, fed, and ready to roll.

They struck the camp quickly and efficiently. Blankets were folded, barrels tied down, and the wheels checked. The road ahead was clear, and with a bit of luck, they'd reach Cookeville before sundown.

Woodrow rode out ahead, scanning the horizon as usual. Not long into the morning's ride, the trail bent gently to the right, revealing dust rising in the distance — another wagon and what looked like a small column of soldiers approaching from the opposite direction.

"Soldiers," David murmured behind him.

Woodrow narrowed his eyes. "Reckon they're just passin' through."

As the groups drew closer, Woodrow slowed his horse, raising one hand in a casual greeting. Ronald, without being told, rode up beside him, flanking the wagon to help guide it around the approaching travelers.

The captain, a sharp-looking man with silver trim on his coat, tipped his hat respectfully toward the women riding in the covered wagon. His gaze lingered just long enough to show manners, then shifted to Woodrow with a firm nod.

"Morning," he said.

"Morning to you," Woodrow replied evenly.

The two parties passed without incident, the rhythmic clop of hooves fading into the distance behind them. But the boys — especially Edward and Merle — were still stealing glances back at the soldiers' uniforms, their curiosity written plain on their faces.

Woodrow turned in his saddle just enough to catch Ronald's eye.

"Keep your eyes forward, son. Closer we get to Cookeville, the thicker the trail traffic's gonna get."

Ronald gave a short nod, adjusting his grip on the reins.

But as the hours wore on, the road remained quiet. The land grew flatter, and soon fences and tilled fields began to appear. Houses dotted the horizon like brushstrokes, and the outlines of buildings in the distance marked the edge of Cookeville.

A sense of arrival settled over the group — not quite relief, but progress. One more town behind them. One step closer to the Territory.

"Stay close now," Woodrow called out. "Let's move through quiet and easy."

The wagon creaked through the edge of town, drawing glances from townsfolk. A few children waved from porches; dogs barked from behind gates. The horses clopped steadily over packed dirt roads, and the scent of hearth smoke mixed with the sharper tang of iron and oil.

Woodrow brought them to a stop in front of the blacksmith's shop — a low building with a soot-darkened chimney and the unmistakable ring of hammer on anvil sounding from within. He dismounted with practiced ease.

"Stretch your legs," he said. "Won't be here long."

A few minutes later, he reappeared from the shop doorway and motioned for Edward and Merle to join him. They jogged over, boots scuffing the dirt.

The blacksmith followed close behind, carrying two heavy pails of axle grease. He handed them off to the boys, nodding once as they took the weight without complaint.

"Take those to Ronald," Woodrow said. "He'll know where to stow 'em."

Business concluded, Woodrow shook the blacksmith's hand — a grip firm and warm, like old friends even if they'd only just met. He turned back to his family.

"Alright now, let's not dawdle. We'll set up camp before the light fades."

As they left town, Woodrow led them down a side trail the blacksmith had mentioned — a narrow cut through the trees that soon opened up to a small clearing beside a spring-fed creek. The water bubbled cold and clear from a mossy outcrop, the sound pure and inviting.

They unpacked quickly, grateful for a chance to stretch and rest. Clara and the girls set about rinsing clothes in the stream, while the boys filled barrels with fresh water. A few teeth-chattering gulps of the icy spring sent laughter echoing through the trees.

"This is good," Woodrow said, mostly to himself as he squatted beside the stream, running water over his face. "Real good."

The fire was lit again by twilight, the sky blushing with the last light of day. Nashville loomed ahead, bigger and busier than any town they'd passed. But for tonight, they had fresh water, safe shelter, and each other.

And that, for a family chasing the promise of a better life, was enough.

Chapter 32
Morning Shadows and Mountain Eyes

As the first rays of sunlight crept over the mossy hills, soft golden light began to break through the thinning fog, casting a gentle glow across the dewy pasture. The land, still wrapped in its sleepy haze, stirred to life under the warmth of dawn. Birds chirped softly overhead, a wood thrush calling out as if to greet the day. The fire in the center of the camp crackled with fresh wood, and the scent of bacon sizzling filled the crisp morning air.

Clara stood at the fire with her trusty old cast-iron skillet—the same one her grandmother had used on a similar open flame generations before. A hundred years of family meals, laughter, and hard times had seasoned that pan better than any oil. Someday, when the time was right, she'd pass it to Mary, just as it had been passed to her. That skillet held stories only the flame could whisper—of prairie lands, snowstorms, and feasts under the stars.

Woodrow returned from tending to the animals, brushing hay from his coat and inhaling deeply as he took in the morning scene. His boots were damp from the dew-covered grass, and his brow was furrowed with quiet concentration. He paused, listening to the distant call of a white-tailed buck warning others of its claim to the land. The fog still hugged the treetops, clinging like a dream that hadn't quite faded. He stood there for a long moment, in awe as always of how nature unfolded with such purpose and rhythm. He believed deeply that there was something holy in how the earth woke up each morning.

Clara noticed him staring out and silently handed him a tin cup of coffee, warm and rich. Her hand lingered on his shoulder for just a second before she turned back to the fire. He accepted the cup with a nod of thanks, eyes still scanning the horizon.

Inside the camp, movement began to stir. David, who had taken the first watch, shifted in his bedroll, dark circles under his eyes from a night of light sleep. Woodrow decided to let the boys sleep just a little longer—he knew the toll of standing guard under the moonlight, listening to every crack of a twig or rustle in the brush.

The fire popped, and the warm smell of fresh bread filled the air. Mary carefully pulled a golden loaf off the stones beside the fire, setting it on a cloth to cool. Clara smiled at her daughter's growing confidence in the kitchen. Meanwhile, Edward quietly grabbed the milk pail and headed toward Lucky, their faithful milk cow, already chewing lazily in the tall grass.

Everyone knew their role without needing to be told. That was something Woodrow took pride in—his family moved like a well-oiled wagon wheel, each part turning smoothly with the others.

By the time Edward returned with a full pail of fresh milk, the rest of the family had gathered around the fire, their faces relaxed, hearts steady in the comfort of each other's company. The fire crackled and popped in rhythm with the morning.

Woodrow glanced at Ronald and gave a short nod—it was his turn to say the blessing. Ronald straightened a little and nodded back. He'd been rehearsing his prayer quietly in his head, knowing his father had asked David the last time.

Ronald bowed his head and cleared his throat.

"Dear Heavenly Father," he began, his voice strong and sincere, *"We thank You for the food we're about to eat, and for watching over us through the night. We ask for Your guidance today and Your protection as we keep heading west. Keep us safe, and keep us strong. Amen."*

Woodrow met his son's eyes afterward, his face softening into a proud smile. He gave him a small nod of approval—a silent acknowledgment between father and son.

After breakfast was cleared and packed away, Woodrow gave quiet instructions.

"David, Ronald, Merle—clean out the water barrels and refill 'em from that cold spring yonder," he said, pointing past the trees.

Clara turned to Edward. "Take the little ones out to the woods and let 'em do their business before we roll out."

"Yes, Ma," Edward replied with a confident air.

He grabbed his new rifle from the wagon, slinging it over his shoulder with a casual but practiced motion. "Never know what might be out there."

He led the younger boys into the woods, keeping an eye out for anything suspicious. His steps were steady, senses alert, just like Pa had taught him. Allen, the youngest, strayed a little behind, gazing up at a noisy woodpecker dancing along a nearby branch, its bright red crest catching the morning sun.

Edward paused, hearing the bird too. He looked up with a grin—until something else caught his eye. Twenty yards beyond Allen, barely visible against the underbrush, was a low, slinking shape.

His stomach dropped.

A mountain lion. Male. Full-grown. Its golden eyes were fixed on Allen. It had been stalking them, and now it was crouched, muscles coiled, tail twitching ever so slightly—ready to pounce.

Edward didn't breathe.

With painstaking slowness, he lifted the rifle off his shoulder. Every second counted. He cocked it gently, just like Pa had shown him. In his mind, he replayed the moment Woodrow took down that massive grizzly not long ago. This had to be the same. Aim steady. Heart calm.

The lion leapt.

CRACK!

The rifle exploded in the morning air.

The echo faded. Everything was still.

Then, a heavy thud.

The lion collapsed mid-leap, skidding to a stop in the leaves just feet from Allen, who sat frozen, eyes wide.

Edward rushed to his brother, heart pounding now, wrapping an arm around him protectively. The little boy clung to him in silence, still stunned.

The other boys had spun around at the gunshot and now stood in shock at what had just happened.

Edward looked down at the fallen beast. He knew that if he hadn't brought that rifle… if he hadn't been watching…

The thought made his knees weak, but he stayed strong for the others.

"That's why we carry," he muttered under his breath.

Mountain Lion Watching

Then, like nothing had happened, Edward stood tall and said firmly, "Let's get back."

As they made their way back to the wagon, Allen still held tightly to his brother's hand. And Edward, rifle in one hand, brother in the other, knew this was a story that would be told around future fires for years to come.

Chapter 33
The Shot That Shook the Hills

Woodrow was tightening the cinch on his saddle when the crack of a rifle shattered the quiet morning air. The sharp sound echoed off the hills like thunder, sending a ripple of tension through the camp.

His heart skipped. One shot. Too close. Too real.

He spun around, his seasoned eyes narrowing toward the direction of the noise. David and Ronald were already tearing across the clearing, rifles in hand, the urgency in their faces mirroring the storm brewing in Woodrow's gut. Without a word, the three of them broke into a sprint, feet pounding against the earth, breath ragged with fear.

As they neared the wooded path, a figure emerged through the veil of trees.

It was Edward—his arms wrapped tightly around little Allen, who clung to his older brother like a cub to its mother. Edward's face was pale, and his eyes were wide, not just from adrenaline but something deeper—guilt, shock, fear.

Woodrow met him halfway. He didn't speak at first. He didn't need to. His arms instinctively reached for Allen, who whimpered and buried his face into his father's chest.

"What happened, son?" Woodrow asked, his voice low but steady. He glanced from Edward to the trees, his mind racing with possibilities.

Edward's mouth opened, but no words came at first. His lips trembled, and his eyes darted down toward the rifle he still clutched in his hand. "I—he—there was a lion, Pa… a mountain lion," he finally managed, the words escaping like wind through cracked glass.

David and Ronald flanked their brother silently, watching their pa's face for a reaction.

Woodrow didn't press him. Not yet. He turned back toward camp with Allen in his arms, Clara already rushing forward, her apron fluttering behind her like a white flag of worry.

"Is he hurt?" she asked, voice brittle with fear as she took her baby into her arms. Together, they inspected Allen from head to toe—scraped knees, a dirty face, but no wounds. No blood. Just wide, frightened eyes and the lingering echo of danger in his tiny body.

"He's fine," Woodrow murmured, brushing a strand of hair from Allen's face. Then he looked up at Edward.

"Come on," he said. "Let's go see."

Edward's breath caught in his throat. Shame burned in his chest like fire. He had almost left the rifle. He had let Allen wander too far. He had frozen when he first saw it. And yet…

He followed his father and brothers in silence. The trail back through the trees seemed shorter this time. His legs were weak, but he pushed forward.

When they reached the clearing, the sight took Woodrow's breath away.

There, lying in the tall grass, was the biggest mountain lion he had ever seen—its body stretched long and thick, muscle and menace even in death. Its golden eyes were still half-open, frozen in a final gaze of hunger and rage. The shot had been clean, right through the eye.

Woodrow walked up slowly, crouched beside the beast. He picked up Edward's rifle from the ground, ran his hand along the stock, then stood. He turned to face his son.

"You held your ground," he said, voice gravel low. "You saved your brother's life."

Edward looked down, still haunted. "I almost didn't. I… I nearly let him die."

Woodrow didn't reply with words. He stepped forward, placed the rifle back in Edward's hands, and wrapped his arms around him in the fiercest bear hug he'd given since they left home.

Edward stiffened at first, then melted into it, overwhelmed by the weight of everything—fear, relief, pride, and the unspoken love between a father and his son.

"You're a man now, Edward," Woodrow said into his ear, voice thick. "You did right."

David and Ronald moved in too, each placing a hand on Edward's shoulder, a nod, a clap on the back, silent warriors offering their respect.

"I reckon we're gonna have to start calling you 'Lion Slayer,'" Ronald grinned, trying to lighten the mood.

Edward chuckled—just barely—but it was the sound of breath returning to the lungs, of a boy who had faced death and done the unthinkable.

They stood there for a long while, just looking at the lion, at the rifle, at each other.

Clara would never know just how close she came to losing her youngest that morning.

But the mountain had taken its shot, and Edward had answered.

And the hills would remember the echo of that single, saving bullet for a long, long time.

Chapter 34
The Heart of the Fire

The light was fading fast over the horizon, bleeding into a dusky purple that kissed the tops of the hills. The air had cooled, and the scent of pine and scorched earth clung to the air around the camp. Woodrow and the boys gathered around the fire, its warm flicker the only defiance against the vast darkness creeping in from the wild.

Mary sat slightly apart from the rest, wrapped in a wool blanket, her back against a thick log. In her arms, little Allen stirred, his breathing soft and shallow, finally easing into the sleep that had eluded him through the trauma of the day. Her face was wet with tears she hadn't even realized had fallen—tears of terror, relief, and something deeper. Love. A fierce, aching love.

To the others, Allen was their youngest brother. But to Mary, he was more than that. She had been there the moment he entered the world—barely thirteen, still a child herself, but that day had changed her. Aunt Annie had called her over, guiding her trembling hands as they cleaned the newborn, the umbilical cord still pulsing, slick with the sacredness of new life. She had swaddled him in cloth, whispered to him softly, and from that moment on, she had felt a quiet ownership of him, like a second mother, sworn by heart if not by birth.

Now, she rocked him gently, pressing her lips to his forehead, her hands trembling as they brushed his hair aside. "You're safe now, baby," she whispered, more to herself than him. "Safe."

Across the fire, Woodrow sat still as stone. His weathered hands rested on his knees, his eyes fixed not on the fire, but on his family—on his daughter and youngest son wrapped in shadow and silence. He saw Clara sitting beside Mary, one hand resting protectively on her daughter's back, her other clutching a folded cloth near her mouth. Her eyes, too, were red with unshed tears.

The flames crackled and snapped, a soft percussion in the quiet reverence that had settled over the camp.

Finally, Woodrow cleared his throat, his voice gravelly from a day held too tightly in his chest.

"Son," he said, directing his voice to Edward, "You've got a big job ahead of you."

Edward looked up from where he sat sharpening his new Bowie knife, his spine straightening instinctively.

"Yes, sir?" he answered, eyes focused, ears listening hard.

"That big cat you killed today… It ain't just a memory. It's a message. That beast came close—too close—to takin' something from us we could never get back." Woodrow looked at Allen then, his jaw tightening. "So we honor the kill. We make use of it."

Edward nodded slowly, waiting.

"I want you to skin that mountain lion," Woodrow continued. "Declaw it. Gut it. Clean it in the spring water—clean enough that your mama'd let you bring it to supper." There was a faint curve at the edge of his lips. "Then we'll stretch it out on top of the wagon to dry. Might be its scent keeps other beasts away. Ain't many things out here willing to mess with a male like that one."

Edward stood, a spark of pride rising in his chest. "Yes, sir. I'll do it right."

"You better," Woodrow said, his voice steady but warm. "That ain't just a chore—it's a rite of passage."

David and Ronald stood with Edward. "We'll help," Ronald said, his voice full of a new kind of admiration for his brother.

"I wanna help too!" piped up Allen suddenly, blinking sleep from his eyes.

Mary held him back gently, but Woodrow raised his hand.

"Let him go," he said.

"Let him be part of it. He earned it the same as the rest."

The boys disappeared into the darkness with torches, their voices fading into the trees as they worked together to honor the kill.

By the time they returned, the lion's pelt had been stripped clean, its massive frame stretched across rough-hewn poles on the wagon's roof. Its claws, like polished ivory, were clutched in the small, dirt-streaked hands of the youngest boys—Allen, RD, and Paul.

They rushed back to the fire, breathless and glowing.

"Look, Pa!" Allen called, his voice proud and bright as he held up a claw that looked nearly half the size of his palm. "I got mine!"

"Me too!" RD grinned, showing his off like a badge.

Woodrow reached forward, inspecting the claws one by one, nodding as he did. "You boys did good."

"You told us to wash 'em up good," said Paul, "So we scrubbed 'til our fingers went numb!"

Clara chuckled, finally breaking her silence, and tousled Paul's hair. "Well, I'm glad you didn't lose your fingers in the process."

Woodrow leaned back against a rock, pulling his pipe from his coat and lighting it slowly. The embers cast a faint orange glow as he exhaled, watching the smoke rise and dissolve into the night air.

Clara moved beside him, tucking her arm beneath his.

"You think they'll ever forget this?" she asked softly.

Woodrow shook his head. "Not a chance."

"They grew today."

"They became men today," he said. "All of 'em."

She rested her head on his shoulder, eyes following the dancing shadows of their children.

Edward sat near the fire, sharpening the claws into pendants, his face focused, proud. Mary and Allen curled beneath a blanket, the little boy now fast asleep once again, tucked safely between her arms. David and Ronald spoke quietly, still a little breathless from the adrenaline of it all. Paul and RD held their claws like treasures, whispering about the next time they'd get to do something so brave.

The fire burned steady, and in the heart of that glowing circle, they weren't just a family. They were a legacy.

Lion Skin

Chapter 35
The Ride to Nashville

The sky was streaked with pale pink and soft gold as dawn broke across the hills, casting long shadows over the campsite. The air was crisp with the scent of pine needles and morning dew, and the crackling of the dying fire whispered the last lullabies of the night.

Edward and the boys had just finished the final task of skinning the great cat. It had been an ordeal—not just a lesson in survival but a bond of blood and bravery, forged between brothers. With steady hands and focused minds, they had worked together, side by side, following Woodrow's instructions to the letter. Now, with the help of their older brothers David and Ron, they hoisted the pelt—the enormous hide still glistening from its cleansing in the cold spring—and began stretching it out atop the wagon.

They moved with quiet reverence, tying down each corner, securing the beast to the sun-bleached planks as though sealing a trophy into legend. From a few paces back, Woodrow watched it all unfold, arms crossed, a glint of pride flashing in his eye. The cat's massive head faced forward, fangs exposed in a permanent snarl as if daring anything in the wild to come close.

The boys gathered near their pa, still catching their breath, their eyes flicking back and forth between the wagon and the approving face of the man they all looked up to.

"Well now…" Woodrow drawled with a satisfied nod, tilting his hat back as he took in the sight. "Looks mighty snazzy, men. Like a war banner. You done good."

Their chests swelled at the praise.

"Alright," he continued, reaching into his coat. "Let's see what ya brought me."

The younger boys, practically vibrating with excitement, stepped forward with outstretched palms. In each small hand were the sharpened claws of the great mountain lion—gleaming, curved talons like nature's own knives. Treasures pulled from the maw of danger. Symbols of courage.

Woodrow pulled a soft leather pouch from his coat pocket—an old tobacco pouch, worn but carefully stitched, saved for something special. "Here ya go, boys," he said, his voice gruff but warm. "Drop 'em in. Got a project in mind for these."

One by one, they placed the claws inside the pouch, each drop sounding with a faint thud against the leather. Paul looked up, his brow furrowed. "What kind of project, Pa?"

Woodrow just smiled, eyes twinkling with mystery. "The kind you don't forget. You'll see."

He tucked the pouch deep into the inside pocket of his coat, close to his chest, like it was sacred. Maybe it was.

Then he turned to his horse, grabbing the reins and swinging up into the saddle in one smooth motion. "Ronald," he called, gesturing toward the wagon, "Let's get movin'. We've got a long road ahead."

Ronald climbed onto the driver's seat and clicked the reins gently. The horses snorted and started forward, their hooves stirring dust into the morning light.

"Nashville," Woodrow said, mostly to himself, but loud enough for them all to hear. "Biggest town we've seen yet. Three, maybe four days' ride if the weather holds and the Lord's willin'."

The boys whooped and hollered behind him, their young hearts beating faster at the thought of the unknown: another journey, another chapter, another story to etch into the scrolls of memory.

Clara watched from her seat inside the wagon, one hand resting on the edge as she looked back toward the horizon they were leaving behind. Mary sat beside her, Allen curled against her shoulder, still sleeping but safe.

Everything was in its place.

And just like that, the wagon rolled forward, creaking in rhythm with the horses' pace. The pelt of the great cat flapped slightly in the breeze above them like a banner of triumph, catching the sun and sending back a golden sheen. A warning to predators. A promise to their future.

They were more than a family now—they were a legend in the making.

And Nashville was waiting.

Chapter 36
Edward's Blessing

The sun was dipping low on the horizon, throwing long shadows across the open trail as the wagon creaked steadily forward. Dust danced behind the horses' hooves, glowing like ash in the amber light of the second day since the mountain lion had been brought down.

But even as the journey pressed on, the air between Woodrow and Edward hung quiet, heavier than usual. In two full days, Edward had barely spoken three words to his pa. He rode with his head bowed, eyes locked somewhere in the dust beneath the wagon wheels, his usual youthful spark dimmed by a storm inside that he hadn't yet named.

Woodrow noticed, of course. A father knows. He could feel the silence like a splinter under the skin. He'd been watching Edward closely, weighing every small movement. It didn't take long to figure it out—Edward was shouldering a weight he didn't know how to carry. He was blaming himself. Somehow, that boy believed the whole encounter with the lion was his fault. Maybe he thought he'd failed in watching his younger brother. Maybe he feared he'd let his pa down by needing to kill the animal at all.

But what Edward couldn't see—what he wasn't yet ready to hear—was the truth that blazed in Woodrow's heart: there was no fault. None. Woodrow saw only bravery, instincts honed by fire, and a boy who'd stepped into the shoes of a man when it mattered most. He couldn't have been prouder.

But boys don't always hear that with words. Sometimes, they need to find it for themselves.

That evening, as golden light gave way to twilight, Woodrow gave a subtle signal from his saddle. Ronald caught it instantly. He was getting better each day at reading his pa without a word—just a glance, a lift of the chin. No need for commands anymore. Ronald guided the wagon off the trail and toward a shaded grove where they'd make camp for the night.

As the family fell into their well-practiced rhythm, the older boys tended to the horses and oxen, checking hooves and refilling troughs, while the younger ones carried buckets of water from a nearby spring. Woodrow took his time inspecting the wagon, teaching as he worked, showing the boys how to feel for loose spokes, grease the axles, and listen for the soft creak that might mean trouble ahead. Every lesson was a seed, planted in the rich soil of responsibility.

By the time the sky turned indigo and stars began to blink to life, the smell of supper had wrapped itself around the camp like a blanket. Clara stood over the cookfire, lifting the lid on the cast-iron pot with a satisfied nod. The aroma of her wilderness stew—rich with foraged herbs, wild onions, and the last of the salted meat—was mouthwatering. Mary sliced up warm, golden cornbread into generous chunks, setting them beside tin plates as steam curled into the night.

The menfolk washed up at the spring, faces pink from the cold water, and took their usual places around the fire. Edward returned last, his boots quiet in the dirt. In one hand, he held a tin jug of fresh milk, cool from the animals. In the other, his hat. He paused before sitting, catching his pa's eyes for the first time all day.

Woodrow met his gaze with a slow nod. "Son," he said, his voice gentle but steady, "Do you mind asking the blessing?"

Edward swallowed, then gave a short nod.

"Yes, sir."

He removed his hat fully and bowed his head. The circle quieted. Even the wind seemed to hush for him.

"God," Edward began, his voice soft but sure, "You must be guardin' each and every one of us… because You've shown Your presence every step of the way. We thank You for providin' our food, our safety, and all the supplies we need… Amen."

The silence that followed wasn't empty. It was full— full of unspoken understanding, of healing, of pride.

Woodrow watched his son, truly looked at him. Thirteen years old and already bearing the weight of manhood with humility and grace, Woodrow saw how he handled that big cat, how he protected his brother… and now this—offering the prayer not just as a chore but as a testimony.

"Thank you, son," Woodrow said, his voice thick with emotion. "Let's eat."

Plates were passed around, cornbread crumbled into stew, and laughter slowly returned to the circle. The tension that had shadowed Edward finally loosened its grip, and for the first time in two days, he smiled. Just a little.

That night, the stars looked especially bright above the campsite, as if even heaven had paused to listen to a young boy step into his calling.

Chapter 37
A Night of Gratitude and Reflection

Woodrow gazed around the campfire, the warmth of the flames flickering against the cool evening air. He was surrounded by the faces of the people he loved most—his family, his rock, his purpose. How different his life would've been without them. It was hard to imagine that kind of loneliness. Lost. Alone. He could only pray that those words would never define his existence. As the fire crackled and popped, Woodrow's thoughts wandered, and for a moment, he let himself feel the depth of the blessing he had been given.

His gaze lingered on Clara, her face lit by the firelight. Nearly twenty years of marriage had passed, and yet, when he looked at her, it felt as though no time had passed at all. She still had that same spark in her eyes—the one that had drawn him in all those years ago. The way her smile lit up her face, the way her laugh echoed in his heart. He was a lucky man, no doubt about it. She had stood by his side through thick and thin, and he knew that, even after all these years, their love only grew stronger.

It wasn't always easy. Clara had endured hardships no mother should have to face—two lost babies in their early years of marriage. Woodrow had never seen a woman grieve the way she had. He knew she carried those losses in her heart, even as their lives continued to move forward. But despite the pain, they had finally been blessed with healthy children, their family growing in ways they had once only dreamed of. Their children were the light of their lives. Woodrow's heart swelled with pride as he watched them play around the camp, their laughter filling the night air. Each day with them was a gift.

He thought about the journey they were on—the long trail they had traveled, the miles stretching out before them. It hadn't been easy. It never was. But every step had led them here, to this moment. They were heading into Nashville tomorrow, the largest town they had seen so far on their travels. Woodrow couldn't help but feel a sense of anticipation. A place like Nashville offered so much—new sights, new opportunities, new faces—and maybe a chance to gather supplies for the next leg of their journey. He had a list in his head of things they'd need: food, tools, and anything else that would make their lives a little easier.

But as he thought about all they might find in Nashville, another thought crossed his mind. The closer they got, the more he realized how much they'd come to rely on each other. How much the simple things—like sharing a meal by the fire or sitting down to talk after a long day—meant. Those moments of connection, of quiet togetherness, were the things that mattered most.

Woodrow looked up at the stars above, feeling a sense of peace settle over him. Nashville was only hours away now. The signs were everywhere—the faint glow of distant lights on the horizon, the sound of animals rustling in the underbrush, the change in the air. It wasn't much longer before they would reach the town. But for now, it was time to rest. He called out to Ronald, who was walking a little further ahead.

"We'll exit the trail here. We'll set up camp for the night and head into town in the morning."

Ronald looked over his shoulder, a grin on his face.

"You always know when it's time to stop, Woodrow. I'll get the fire started."

Woodrow nodded. "Yeah, no point in rushing. Nashville can wait 'til tomorrow. For now, let's enjoy the night and have a good meal." He turned to his family, his eyes scanning the group as his children scattered to gather firewood.

Clara, busy over the fire preparing their supper, glanced up and gave him a smile that made his heart ache with affection.

"Dinner will be ready soon," she said.

"You should sit down and relax for once, Mr. 'Let's get everything done.'"

Woodrow chuckled, sitting down on a nearby log and stretching his legs.

"I'll relax when we're all settled. But you're right, I could use a minute. How's everything going with the stew?"

"It's almost ready," Clara replied with a wink.

"And don't think I've forgotten that you promised me a special anniversary dinner once we get settled in Nashville."

He laughed, the sound rich with fondness.

"Can't wait. You know I'll do whatever it takes to make it special."

Their daughter, Paul, ran up to Woodrow, his arms full of sticks.

"Look, Papa, I found the biggest one!" he said, his face beaming with pride.

Woodrow grinned and ruffled his hair.

"Well done, little one. You're becoming a fine firewood gatherer."

His heart swelled as he looked at him, at all of them. They were his world.

The fire crackled, and their youngest son, Allan, wandered over, sitting down beside his father.

"Papa, do you think Nashville will have any good toys?" he asked with a hopeful look in his eyes.

Woodrow smiled warmly at his son.

"Maybe, Allan. But the real treasure in Nashville is what we find together, not what we buy. We're a family, and that's all we need."

Allan seemed to consider that for a moment before nodding slowly.

"I like that."

Clara looked over at Woodrow, her eyes soft with affection.

"I'm glad we have this time together. I don't know what I would do without you all."

She placed a hand on his shoulder, and he leaned into it, feeling the quiet strength of their bond.

Woodrow reached out and squeezed her hand.

"I don't think I'd be able to go on without you. We've been through a lot, but every step, every hard moment, has led us here. To this."

Clara smiled, her eyes twinkling in the firelight.

"To here, to now, and to all the good that's still ahead."

"Exactly," he agreed.

The firelight flickered between them, casting long shadows across the ground. The world beyond their little circle seemed distant, almost irrelevant. For tonight, they were home, in each other's company, and that was enough.

He looked up at the stars, feeling the weight of everything they had faced and everything that lay ahead.

"Tomorrow, we'll head into Nashville. But tonight…" He paused, taking a deep breath, "Tonight, we're here. And that's all that matters."

Clara placed a bowl of hot stew in his hands, and he looked up at her with a grateful smile.

"Thank you, Clara. For everything."

She smiled back, her face aglow in the firelight.

"You're welcome, Woodrow. Now, let's eat."

The night stretched on, peaceful and full of warmth. Their laughter echoed into the quiet, the crackling of the fire the only other sound. Tomorrow could wait. For now, they had each other, and that was all that mattered.

Chapter 38
The Guns of Nashville

After a restful night and a hearty breakfast, the wagon rumbled down the dusty road with Nashville in sight. The excitement in the air was palpable, but Woodrow's voice cut through the chatter like a sharp blade.

"Keep the animals tight, boys. The town's a madhouse, and we're not here for sightseeing. Watch everyone and everything around us."

His tone was steady and commanding. The boys nodded and tightened the reins, their eyes sharp and aware. They were used to Woodrow's serious demeanor—it was his way of making sure no one ever let their guard down. The closer they got to the bustling town, the more Woodrow's instincts kicked in. The city was full of risks, and it was his job to keep them safe.

"We'll hit the blacksmith first," Woodrow continued, "Then the general store for supplies. Stay with the wagon and inside while I take care of things."

The horses snorted softly as they trotted, the road ahead becoming more crowded with each mile. Woodrow gave a brief nod to the boys and then stepped down from the wagon, his boots kicking up dust as he strode toward the blacksmith's shop.

The sound of hammering metal greeted him as he entered the workshop. A large man with a grizzled beard looked up from his forge, wiping his brow with a cloth. He extended his hand with a firm grip.

"I'm Woodrow," he said, shaking the blacksmith's hand.

"Bob," the man replied with a nod.

"How can I help you, my friend?"

Woodrow wasted no time.

"We need a couple of tubes of grease and some clean water. And what about a gun shop?"

Bob's face lit up with a knowing smile.

"I can help you with the grease, no problem. And there's a well down by the general store, at the end of the street."

Woodrow's eyes narrowed, the wheels turning in his head.

"Thanks, Bob. But the gun shop, where is it?"

"The gunsmith's shop is about a hundred yards down the road on the right," Bob replied, his voice low.

"Look for the sign that reads 'Adam's Guns and Ammunition.'"

Woodrow gave a nod of appreciation and paid for the grease, placing it in the wagon. Then he turned back to the boys, his voice steady as he spoke.

"There's a gun shop on the right, boys. Stop at the sign that says Adam's Guns."

They continued down the street, the sounds of the city growing louder. As they reached the gun shop, Woodrow called for everyone to get out of the wagon.

"Take a break, boys. Water the animals," he said as they stretched their legs. Woodrow then made his way into the gun shop, his presence immediately commanding attention. The boys followed, their eyes wide at the sight of the shop— a haven for anyone looking for weapons. Rifles and pistols hung from every wall, in racks and display cases. The air was thick with the smell of metal and leather.

Woodrow approached the counter where an older man stood, examining a rifle. He nodded toward a Colt 45 hanging behind the counter.

"I'd like to see that one," Woodrow said, his voice firm but friendly.

The man behind the counter pulled down the revolver, handing it over to Woodrow with a small smile.

Woodrow slipped the Colt out of its holster, feeling the weight of it in his hand. It was perfect. He checked the barrel, the grip, the balance, and then gave it a satisfied nod.

"I'll take it," he said, turning to the man.

"And throw in five hundred shells."

David, his eldest son, watched his father closely. With a grin, he approached the counter, his eyes scanning the rows of pistols.

Woodrow gestured to a similar model beside his own Colt.

"What do you think, son?"

David smiled at his father, his eyes full of pride. He took the gun in his hands, inspecting it just like Woodrow had. After a moment, he nodded and looked at his father again.

"This one's mine," he said firmly.

Ronald stepped up next, just like his older brother. He chose the same model, following his father's example. Woodrow's pride swelled as he watched his sons—each of them growing into capable men, ready for anything.

"Okay, Edward," Woodrow said, turning to his youngest, a tall thirteen-year-old already pushing six feet two.

"Your turn. Make sure it fits right. You don't want a gun too heavy for you."

Edward stood taller than most men at his age, but he was still growing. He carefully tried on a holster, adjusting it around his waist to make sure the weight was manageable. After a few moments, he nodded to his father, signaling that he'd found the right one.

Woodrow's eyes softened. Edward had proven himself time and time again, especially during their travels. It was time for him to carry a man-sized weapon.

Woodrow's voice grew steady as he gave his final command.

"Strap them on, boys. They stay on from now until you lie down to sleep. I'll explain why later."

The boys nodded, understanding the gravity of their father's words. They slipped on their holsters, the weight of the guns settling comfortably against their sides.

Woodrow watched them for a moment, pride swelling in his chest. "You're not boys anymore. You're men, and this is how we stay safe."

The shopkeeper nodded in approval, sensing the change in the air. "It'll do you well," he said gruffly.

"A good pistol's a man's best friend in a place like Nashville."

Woodrow gave a final glance around the shop, then turned to his sons, who were adjusting their weapons with the careful precision they had been taught.

"Alright, let's go. We've got work to do."

As they exited the shop, Woodrow could see it in their eyes—the same fire that burned in his own. They were ready for whatever lay ahead. And with their new pistols at their sides, they would face the challenges of Nashville together.

The streets of the city buzzed with activity, but Woodrow knew this was only the beginning. There were more steps to take, and more lessons to learn, but for now, his boys had their first real taste of responsibility.

And that would make all the difference.

Chapter 39
Colts and Lessons

Woodrow and the boys walked proudly with their new Colts. Woodrow had struck a deal at the gun shop, paying $60 for four new Colt 45s, a deal that cost him more than he usually spent, but one that was necessary for the journey ahead. The price was high, but he'd planned ahead, knowing the journey's expenses, and he had carefully thought out how to manage their remaining resources after selling nearly everything they owned.

As they walked back to the wagon, Woodrow told the boys that once they were alone, he would explain his reasoning behind the new guns. The boys nodded, eager to learn more.

Clara, noticing the new Colt 45s strapped to their waists, looked at Woodrow with an expression that spoke volumes—one he hadn't seen in a long time. He reassured her, "I'll explain later when the time is right."

They reached the general store, where Woodrow signaled for the boys to gather water. Clara mentioned that she and the younger children were heading inside to shop and that they had plenty of money left over from the last time he had given them a couple of gold coins. Woodrow tipped his hat, telling her they would be waiting by the wagon.

While the boys filled the barrels with water, Woodrow took a moment to explain the importance of their new weapons.

"Men, the reason we have these Colts," he began, "Is because the land between Nashville and the West is dangerous. Outlaws tend to prey on families heading west, and if they see that we're armed, wearing the same kind of guns, it might make them think twice before messing with us."

He looked at Edward and added, "Little brother, there's another reason we have to stay alert. You'll all be able to shoot like professionals before we reach the Territory."

The boys looked at each other, their admiration for their pa growing deeper. Woodrow had always made them feel like they were men, trusted to protect their family. Once the water barrels were full and the rest of the family returned to the wagon, they were ready to move on to the next town, Memphis.

Chapter 40
Storm on the Horizon

The heavy wagon, now loaded with fresh supplies from the general store, rumbled forward toward Memphis, a long stretch of road ahead. Woodrow's mind was focused on the journey ahead, estimating that it would take them around nine days to reach their destination. However, what caught his attention more than the miles ahead were the boys.

They seemed different now. They sat a little straighter in their saddles, their faces more serious, as though the weight of the new Colts on their hips had aged them overnight. The way they held themselves, no longer children but young men, was evident. Woodrow couldn't help but feel a sense of pride, knowing he had prepared them for whatever lay ahead. But there was also a heaviness in his heart—he knew the dangers they would face and the new responsibility each of them had taken on by wearing a gun at their sides.

What they didn't know, however, was what the blacksmith had told him in town. Woodrow hadn't shared it with them, or even with Clara. As he drove the wagon along, he thought back to the conversation. The blacksmith had pointed to the hide of a large mountain lion, stretched out across the top of the wagon.

"Folks around here have been losing livestock to these cats," the blacksmith had said, his voice low.

"One man was attacked about a month ago. He barely escaped with his life. His son scared the big cat off with a shot, but the man had a good look at it. Said it had an ear nearly torn off, like it had been in a fight."

The blacksmith's words weighed on Woodrow's mind. He confirmed what he'd suspected when they'd killed the lion. The blacksmith had even gone on to say that they'd done a good thing, removing such a dangerous animal from the area. Woodrow had planned to tell the family at supper, around the fire, but not now—right now, they needed to focus on the storm.

The air around them thickened as the wind picked up, signaling that a storm was on the way. Woodrow scanned the sky; the dark clouds loomed like a curtain about to drop. He could feel the change in the atmosphere, the weight of it pressing down on him. A storm was coming, and they needed to find shelter before it hit.

"Alright, we need to set up camp fast," Woodrow said, his voice firm. "The storm's coming, and we can't be out in the open when it hits."

He turned to Ronald, his oldest boy, and motioned for him to follow.

"You stay close. We need to find a good spot to camp— somewhere we can get cover from the wind and rain."

The boys were quick to react. They followed Woodrow off the main trail, seeking out a sheltered spot. Woodrow's eyes darted around, assessing the landscape, until he found a place at the foot of a hillside—an area that would offer the protection they needed.

"Here!" he called, pointing to the spot.

"We'll set up here."

The family jumped into action, moving with practiced efficiency. They had done this countless times before, but this storm felt different. The air was heavy with anticipation, and the wind was already picking up. Woodrow and Ronald hurried to tie the draft horses to a pair of sturdy hickory trees, securing them before the storm could make things difficult. David and the younger boys did the same with the other animals, hurrying to shelter them as best as they could.

David and Edward grabbed the heavy tarps, working together to spread them across the wagon and secure them with ropes. The wind whipped around them, and the rain came down in sheets, cold and biting. Woodrow helped with the last of the tarps, pulling hard on the ropes to fasten them tightly just as the storm began to unleash its fury.

"Stay low!" Woodrow shouted to the boys as he motioned for them to hold on tightly to the sides of the wagon. The sound of the wind was deafening now, almost like the growl of a wild animal.

Inside the wagon, Clara and the younger children huddled together for warmth, trying to stay dry as the storm battered the outside. The older boys stood at the edge of the wagon, gripping the sides as the wind tried to tear at the tarps. The rain turned to hail, sharp and cold, the stones pelting the animals and the wagon alike. The horses, frightened by the chaos, tugged at their tethers, desperate to escape the storm.

"Hold tight!" Woodrow shouted over the roar of the wind.

"Stay down! We've got a twister coming in!"

His voice barely carried over the storm, but the urgency in his tone was clear. The trees around them groaned under the pressure of the wind, some already snapping and crashing to the ground. Woodrow could feel the ground beneath him tremble, and he knew the tornado was close.

The family huddled together, trying to make themselves as small as possible in the face of nature's fury. The storm's intensity was like nothing they'd encountered on the trail so far. It felt as though their time on the road, which had been relatively smooth up until now, was about to be tested in the most dangerous way.

Woodrow's eyes scanned the horizon, and he knew that they had to act fast. They were at the mercy of the storm, and they couldn't let their guard down. This was no longer just about finding shelter from rain—it was about survival. The twister was coming, and he had no idea how bad it would be, but he wasn't about to let his family face it without being prepared.

As the storm raged around them, Woodrow's thoughts turned to the mountain lion and the warning the blacksmith had given. The West was full of dangers—animals, outlaws, and nature itself. But as long as they had each other, Woodrow knew they could face whatever came their way.

Chapter 41
The Storm

Woodrow could feel the tension in the air as the storm's fury grew. The wind howled like a beast, whistling through the trees, bending the branches until they creaked and groaned under the pressure. He could see the dark clouds swirling above them, churning in a way that sent a chill down his spine. The boys, drenched to the bone, huddled close, their faces set in grim determination, but Woodrow's heart was heavy with fear for them all.

The rain pounded down in sheets, stinging their skin like needles, and the hail began to batter them from all directions. It was relentless, icy, and sharp, hitting with such force it felt as though it might pierce their very souls. The tarp above them, once a comforting shield, was now a nightmare in the making. It flapped violently in the wind, its edges pulling free from the stakes that had once held it securely in place. Woodrow's eyes darted between the boys, his mind working quickly, assessing their situation. The storm wasn't just fierce—it was becoming a full-blown twister.

"Boys!" Woodrow shouted, his voice barely audible over the howling wind.

"It's gonna be on us in a minute or two—stay close!"

Before the boys could react, the tarp tore loose completely, and with a deafening crack, it whipped wildly in the wind, threatening to tear apart in front of their eyes. Woodrow's instincts kicked in, and without thinking, he grabbed the boys by the arms and dragged them under the wagon.

"Now, under the wagon, quick!" Woodrow shouted.

They scrambled beneath the safety of the wagon just as the world seemed to fall apart around them. The sound of the storm was deafening, like a thousand freight trains roaring overhead. But then, just as suddenly as it had started, the wind ceased. The storm, for a brief moment, held its breath.

Everything went still.

Woodrow lay motionless, his heart racing as he listened intently. His breath came in shallow gasps, and for the first time in what seemed like an eternity, the only sound was the distant rumble of the storm's aftermath. The rain had slowed to a steady drizzle, but the air was thick with the remnants of the chaos that had just passed over them.

"Stay still," Woodrow whispered urgently to the boys, his eyes scanning their faces for any sign of panic. When he was sure they were all okay, he slowly eased himself out from beneath the wagon. His boots sank into the mud as he moved toward the wagon's edge, peering out into the darkness.

He needed to check on Clara and see if she and the others were alright. Woodrow's breath caught as he saw her and Mary crouched down, their faces pale with fear. They were safe, but he could see the terror in their eyes. He reached them quickly, his hands steady but his heart pounding.

"It's over now," he said, his voice soft but firm.

"The worst of it has passed."

Clara let out a shaky breath, her arms trembling as she stood and hugged him tightly. Mary did the same, and for a moment, Woodrow allowed himself to hold them both. He could feel the weight of their fear, and he knew it was his strength they needed now more than ever. He'd kept them alive through the storm, but there was more to do.

"Boys," Woodrow said, his voice regaining its usual authority.

"Let's check on the animals. Make sure everyone's alright."

The boys nodded and quickly scrambled to their feet, moving toward the makeshift corral. They checked each animal one by one, their hands gentle but thorough. None of the animals were lost or hurt. Even the hounds, who had been tethered nearby, had weathered the storm with the boys, staying close and steady despite the chaos.

When Woodrow was sure the animals were safe, he turned his attention to the wagon. It had taken a beating from the storm, but it was still intact. The tarp, however, had to be repaired before it would offer any protection again. Together, they worked quickly to fix it, their hands steady despite the exhaustion that weighed heavily on them.

As they finished, Woodrow looked out toward the horizon. The twister had passed overhead, and in its wake, the destruction was evident. Far off in the distance, he could see the marks it had left—trees uprooted, debris scattered across the land, the unmistakable sign of a storm that had torn through with deadly force.

"We're lucky," Woodrow muttered to himself, though he knew it wasn't just luck that had kept them safe. It had been quick thinking, determination, and the strength of everyone working together.

"Alright, boys," Woodrow said, his voice strong again.

"Let's round up some firewood. We'll need to get a fire going before it gets too dark. We'll have to use some lantern fuel to get it started, but we'll manage."

Clara, Mary, and the boys gathered around Woodrow, their faces drawn but grateful. They wrapped their arms around him, their silent gestures of appreciation saying more than words ever could. Woodrow could feel the weight of the day in their embrace, the exhaustion that had settled deep into their bones. But he was proud of them—of how they had all pulled through.

As the fire crackled to life, Clara lit a lantern, and Mary followed suit, preparing the cooking skillets. The warmth of the flames pushed back the chill of the storm, and the soft light from the lanterns created a small, comforting circle in the midst of the wild night.

Today had been long. Today had been terrifying. But in the end, they had survived. They had done what they had to do to make it through. And as the darkness settled around them, Woodrow couldn't help but feel a glimmer of hope. They had faced the storm, and they had come out the other side, together.

Chapter 42
A Prayer for the Journey

The fire crackled softly in the darkness, casting flickering shadows that danced across the faces of those gathered around it. Woodrow and Clara sat side by side, their eyes scanning the faces of their children, now grown strong and healthy. Eight of them. Eight children they had raised in that old cabin back home, through years of hard work, sacrifice, and love. And yet, as they sat there on this cold night, they couldn't shake the terror they had felt just hours before. The storm had come upon them with a ferocity that had left them breathless, but they had survived.

In a heartbeat, they could have lost everything—every one of their children, their home, their lives. But by some miracle, by the hand of God, they had been spared. Woodrow's chest tightened as he thought of the Almighty's protection. It was a feeling that settled deep within him, humbling him in ways words couldn't describe.

Looking around at the faces of the children he had fought so hard to raise, Woodrow felt a mixture of gratitude and awe. The Almighty's hand had been on them, guiding them, protecting them. It wasn't luck. No, this was something far greater.

"Clara," he murmured quietly, his voice thick with emotion, "The Lord has had His hands on us today, hasn't He?"

Clara nodded without saying a word, her face reflecting the same quiet reverence. She reached out and took his hand, a silent gesture of unity in the face of the storm's wrath.

It was supper time, and as they sat there, the warmth of the fire and the comfort of full bellies helped to ease some of the tension that still hung in the air. But Woodrow knew it was time. It was time to pray.

He waited for everyone to settle, for the sounds of laughter and chatter to die down. The children—some of them young men now, others still with the innocence of youth—gathered close, their attention on him. They all knew their father well enough by now to understand when something important was coming. This wasn't just another night around the fire.

Woodrow cleared his throat, his voice carrying over the crackling of the fire as he spoke.

"Let's pray."

He bowed his head, and the others followed suit.

"Lord, I know now for sure that You're in control of everything. And even though we don't deserve any of Your blessings, I'm so obliged to You for sparing our lives tonight. We thank You, Lord, for the food the ladies have provided on this dark and weary night. You've shown us mercy, and for that, we're grateful. In Your name, Amen."

The words hung in the air, heavy with gratitude, awe, and recognition. When he finished, the silence that followed was sacred. Each person reflected on the blessing of that prayer, on the quiet miracle that had unfolded in their midst.

The storm had passed, but it was clear that something deeper had shifted inside each of them.

After everyone had eaten, the plates and skillets were cleaned and put away, and the fireside grew quieter. Woodrow could see the questions in their eyes, the curiosity in their gazes. It was time.

"I've got a few things to say to all of you," he said, his voice steady, carrying a sense of weight and finality.

The older boys exchanged knowing glances. They had been around long enough to understand when their father was about to share something serious. Woodrow had always been a man of few words, but when he spoke, it mattered. They leaned in closer, hanging on every word.

Woodrow shifted his weight and stared into the fire for a moment as if gathering the strength to speak what was in his heart.

"We just dodged a bullet today," he began, his voice low but clear.

"That storm… it could have ended us. But we're here. We made it through. And that's not just luck. The Almighty's hand was on us, and we owe Him everything for that."

He paused, letting the weight of his words sink in. The air was heavy with expectation as his children waited for him to continue.

Woodrow wiped a hand across his face, exhaustion creeping into his bones as he spoke again.

"But that was just the beginning. I've had some long talks with the blacksmith and the gun shop owner in town. They both told me the same thing—this journey ahead of us, it's gonna be hard. Real hard. And when we get to Memphis and cross that Mississippi River, things are gonna get even worse."

The boys exchanged nervous glances, understanding the direction of this conversation. They knew what it meant when their father talked like this.

"Beyond that river, the land's different," Woodrow continued, his voice growing more resolute.

"We're heading into the Arkansas Territory. And that's a place where the law don't hold much weight. It's the land of outlaws, thieves, and lawless men. Men who'll stop at nothing to take what they want."

A somber silence fell over the group as the gravity of his words settled over them. They were heading into the unknown, and the danger they would face was as real as the ground beneath their feet.

"That's why," Woodrow said, his eyes locking with each of his sons, "we're carrying these Colts. We've all got one now, and by the time we hit that Territory, we'll be experts with these pistols. I'm telling you now, no one—no one—will mess with us. We've got the means to protect what's ours, and we will."

He paused again, allowing the weight of what he was saying to sink in. His eyes softened slightly as he looked around at his family, his heart swelling with love and pride.

"The men in town warned me, especially about taking my family through there alone. They told me we'd be a target. Outlaws would see us as easy pickings. But they'll be wrong. We won't be easy. We won't be prey."

Woodrow's voice grew firm, his words carrying the resolve of a man who had seen enough in his life to know the cost of survival.

"The Lockharts don't give up. We don't back down. And we sure as hell don't let anyone disrespect us. We'll stand tall, we'll protect each other, and we'll keep moving forward. The storm might have passed, but we're about to face a whole new kind of challenge."

His sons nodded, their faces set with determination. Woodrow could see the fire in their eyes—the same fire that had burned in him for years, the drive to protect his family, to keep them safe against all odds.

"Tomorrow," he said, standing tall and firm, "We keep pushing forward. We don't stop. We don't falter. The road ahead is uncertain, but we're Lockharts. And that means we don't quit. We make our own fate."

The fire crackled and popped, sending a shower of sparks into the night sky. The world around them may have been dark and dangerous, but in that moment, the family felt an unspoken bond, a unity that no storm, no matter how fierce, could ever break.

Chapter 43
The Morning of Change

The morning light broke over the horizon, casting a warm glow across the land as Woodrow gathered his boys around him after a simple breakfast. The air was cool and crisp, and the family could feel the weight of what lay ahead. Woodrow's voice carried a calm confidence, the kind that came from years of knowing the land and the challenges it presented.

"Boys," he said, his voice steady, "This day will be different from now on. Today, we prepare."

Clara and Mary, along with the younger boys, stood by, watching with a mixture of curiosity and concern. Woodrow's face was serious, the fire of determination in his eyes. This wasn't just about training; it was about survival, about securing their future in a land that offered no guarantees. The boys looked to him with a mixture of respect and eagerness, knowing that today would mark the beginning of something crucial.

"Alright, men," Woodrow continued, "After breakfast, we'll be practicing with those pistols of yours. We're not worrying about speed right now—only accuracy. Accuracy is the key to survival, and you'll need it when we head into the unknown."

He led them to an open clearing, where an old, sturdy tree stood tall about 40 feet away. The trunk was a solid foot across, its bark rough and weathered. Woodrow had a plan in mind. He walked toward the tree, his boots crunching the earth beneath them, and began tying a grease bucket to the tree.

"Five feet up," he said, securing the rope with a practiced hand.

"That's the target. Focus on it, and hit it square in the middle. Let's see what you've got."

The boys took out their Colts, their hands steady but their minds full of questions. Woodrow's calm presence was a stark contrast to the tension in the air. He looked at each of his sons, seeing in their eyes the same determination that had once filled him when he was their age. Today wasn't just about shooting; it was about teaching them a skill that would keep them alive.

Woodrow stepped forward first, the weight of his old pistol familiar in his hand. It wasn't the same as when he'd first held it, but it felt right. He raised it to eye level, closing his left eye, his right hand steady on the grip. He took a breath, aimed carefully at the middle of the bucket, and pulled the trigger.

The sound of the shot cracked through the still morning air, loud and deafening. The boys jumped at the force of it, their hearts racing. The bucket flipped in mid-air, swinging violently but staying tied to the tree. They all ran to the tree to inspect the shot. Woodrow was the last to reach it, and when he saw the hole, his heart swelled with pride. He had hit the bucket square in the center, the hole large enough to fit his thumb in. It was a perfect shot.

"That's how you do it, boys," Woodrow said, his voice low but filled with pride.

"Accuracy is the key. Now, David, it's your turn. Aim at the hole in the bucket, son."

David stepped up with a determined look, his hands steady as he aimed his Colt at the target. He took a deep breath, recalling his father's calmness, the steadiness of his stance. The shot rang out, and the boys rushed to the tree. David had hit just above his father's shot, almost perfectly in line with it. It wasn't a direct hit, but it was close—very close. The boys murmured in approval.

"Nice shot, son," Woodrow said, his voice filled with a quiet pride.

"Ronald, you're up."

Ronald stepped forward eagerly, eager to make his mark. He mimicked his father's stance, keeping calm and focusing on the target. The shot rang out, and they hurried to the tree. His hole was left of David's, but still impressive—another solid shot.

Edward was up next, his excitement barely contained.

"I'm gonna do better than my brothers," he muttered under his breath, though his voice carried no arrogance—just determination. He raised the pistol slowly, taking his time. He aimed carefully, breathing in the morning air, and then fired.

The sound of his shot echoed across the clearing. When they reached the tree, they saw that his shot had landed just beneath his father's. Not perfect, but still impressive for his first try.

Woodrow looked at his sons with pride in his heart.

"That's enough," he said, his voice firm yet full of admiration.

"With just one shot, I've seen enough. You're all ready. You did exactly what I wanted. Calm, focused, accurate. That's what will keep us alive out here."

He holstered his Colt and turned toward the road ahead.

"Let's roll, boys. Memphis is our next stop."

The journey ahead was uncertain, but with his sons at his side, Woodrow knew they were as ready as they could be.

The family gathered their things, the younger boys still buzzing with excitement at their success, while Clara and Mary exchanged knowing glances. They were heading into a world that was wild and untamed, but together, they were strong. Woodrow knew it wasn't just about the pistols in their hands—it was about the strength in their hearts and the unity of their family. And in that moment, as they set their sights on the road ahead, he knew they would face whatever came their way, together.

Chapter 44
Crossing Paths with the Law

Woodrow gathered everyone around the wagon and told them that, from now on, they'd all have to stay very alert—and speak up if they noticed anything out of place. He nodded at the older boys and gave them a sign to watch for: if they ever saw him take out his rifle and rest it on his lap, pointed at the sky, that meant to be ready for anything and get their rifles out.

"I'll handle anyone approaching us from the front," Woodrow said.

"If they want to talk, I'll do the talking. I'll count on you boys to keep an eye on the rear. Don't let anyone sneak up on us.

They all nodded.

"Yes, sir," they replied in unison.

"We've got a little more than a week before we reach Memphis. Once there, we'll make it a quick stop and catch a steamboat to cross the Mississippi River."

The next three days went by smoothly—they didn't see a soul.

But as they got closer to Memphis, the road grew busier. They saw riders and wagons coming and going from town. Suddenly, David signaled Ronald to stop the wagon and grab his rifle—he had seen the sign. Woodrow's rifle was resting across his lap, barrel pointed to the sky. Everyone moved closer to the wagon to stay near their mother and younger siblings inside.

Woodrow lowered his rifle as a man approached. He was accompanied by five other riders, all dressed in long black coats and black hats. Woodrow exchanged a few words with the man before turning back and motioning for David to join him.

As David walked up, he noticed all six riders wore badges—U.S. Marshals.

Woodrow shook hands with their leader, Marshal Andrew "Heck" Thomas, a lawman known across the country as one of the best. David stepped up beside his pa, shook the Marshal's hand, and nodded politely. The deputies acknowledged both of them in kind.

Marshal Thomas pulled three wanted posters from his coat and asked if they had seen anyone matching the descriptions along the trail. Woodrow shook his head no.

He then waved Ronald forward, and the rest of the family gathered closer.

Marshal Thomas adjusted his massive black mustache as he studied the group. Leaning in closer to Woodrow, he said, "Now I know who you folks are. You're famous all the way to the Territory and Dodge City, Kansas. They call you the '*Lion Killer Family.*' When I saw that big cat stretched out on top of your wagon, I knew."

Woodrow turned toward Edward and gave him a look. The Marshal followed his gaze, nodded at Edward, and smiled.

"Son, when you're a few years older, I'd like to have you as a deputy."

He looked around at the family.

"You don't know how much the folks appreciated you taking down that big cat. It's been terrifying the area for years."

"Well, Mr. Lockhart," he added, tipping his hat, "We'd best be moving on. Got some outlaws to round up. Looks like you're in good hands—with a fine crew here."

As they rode off, the Marshal called back, "Keep your Colts strapped on, young men. Every towns got its own story."

The Marshal and his deputies tipped their hats to the ladies as they passed and continued down the trail.

Lion Skin

Chapter 45
The Warning Shot

Woodrow slowed the team and brought the wagon to a complete halt just before the road fed into the main part of town. He reined in the horses carefully, his eyes scanning the chaotic scene ahead where wagons and riders moved with a wild disregard for order.

Turning to Clara, he asked in a steady voice, "What all do we need at the general store?"

Clara, already prepared, reached under the wagon seat and pulled out a folded piece of paper.

"I made a list," she said, handing it over. Woodrow nodded approvingly.

"We'll make this fast," he said.

"I want us across that river and on the steamboat before dark settles in."

Clara understood the urgency without needing further explanation. She called over her shoulder to Edward.

"Come on, son. You're helping me."

Then she turned to Mary and added firmly, "You stay here with the little boys and watch over them."

Mary, dutiful and calm, nodded and gathered the younger boys close, preparing to wait in the wagon while Clara and Edward headed for the store.

Woodrow reminded them all of the plans that the Marshal had laid out earlier.

"Marshal Thomas told me where everything is. We don't need to be asking around or wasting time. The first stop is the blacksmith's for supplies, then we head to the freshwater well down the street, and the general store is right across from the well. Keep your heads down and stay sharp."

The wagon creaked forward again, entering the disorder of Memphis. Compared to Nashville, this place was wilder and rougher. Wagons barreled down the middle of the streets without care, kicking up dust and forcing others aside. Riders raced each other recklessly, hooting and hollering as they weaved between pedestrians and horses alike. It was a city full of noise, movement, and danger.

Woodrow made a quick trip into the blacksmith's shop and came back out in no time, carrying a tin of axle grease for the wagon.

Meanwhile, Clara and Edward moved swiftly through the general store. When they emerged, their arms were full—sacks of flour, salt, lamp oil, dried beans, and bolts of cloth stacked precariously.

Seeing the load they carried, Woodrow waved toward Merle and RD.

"Go help your ma with the sacks," he ordered.

The two boys jumped down and hurried to assist, taking some of the heavier supplies from Clara's arms. Across the way, Ronald and David were working just as efficiently, nearly finished loading the barrels of fresh water onto the back of the wagon.

Everything was going exactly as Woodrow had planned—tight, quick, and without a hitch—until a sudden interruption jolted them off course.

As Mary stepped down to help load one of the lighter bundles, a cowboy—dusty, loud, and riding loose in his saddle—spotted her. He trotted up, a grin splitting his face.

"Hey, Missy!" he shouted, his voice thick and mocking.

"How 'bout you go for a little ride with me?"

Mary turned to face him, her expression polite but firm.

"No, thank you," she said clearly.

"We're leaving."

But the cowboy wasn't finished.

Leaning forward in his saddle, he reached toward the draft horses, snatching one of the leather straps tied to the wagon brake. His hand gripped the strap firmly as he sneered.

"I believe you didn't hear me right," he said.

"You're coming for a ride with me."

The words barely left his mouth when Woodrow reacted.

He heard the cowboy's taunt and in a flash, he was around the wagon, mounted and moving, Colt .45 drawn and held low at his side. His expression was grim, his whole body radiating cold, steady anger.

At the same moment, Clara was already moving.

Without hesitation, she cocked the double-barrel shotgun and leveled it at the cowboy's chest, her stance firm, her aim unwavering.

Chapter 46
The Weight of Reputation

Now, every Lockhart had a Colt .45 drawn and aimed squarely at the cowboy who had been causing trouble. Their faces were like stone, unwavering and silent, making it clear they were ready to defend their own.

A few of the cowboys' companions sat farther down the street, watching the scene unfold. They shifted nervously in their saddles, clearly realizing their drunk friend was making a fool of himself—and possibly getting himself into real trouble.

Woodrow guided his horse in closer at a slow, deliberate pace. When he was within a few feet of the cowboy, he raised his pistol slightly, pointing it directly toward the man's face. His voice was cold and steady as he said,

"Cowboy, you might want to let go of that strap and go on—mind your own business."

The cowboy wavered for a moment, his whiskey-soaked brain trying to process the danger he had stumbled into.

Before he could make another foolish move, two of his friends rode up quickly from the group in the distance. Dust kicked up around them as they pulled their horses to a stop.

One of the cowboys, a wiry man who seemed slightly more sober than the rest, lifted his hand in a peaceable gesture and addressed Woodrow respectfully.

"Sir," he said, tipping his hat, "We'll take care of our friend here and make sure he doesn't act out again."

He glanced toward the wagon, noting the distinctive cat-skin banner draped across the top, and then at the grim, ready faces of the Lockhart sons.

"From the looks of your sons—and that cat skin on your wagon top—we know now who you are. We're real sorry, sir. It won't happen again."

Woodrow held his gaze for a long, heavy moment, weighing the sincerity of the man's words.

Finally, with a slight nod, he accepted the apology.

He watched carefully as the drunk cowboy was gathered up and escorted away by his friends, their horses kicking up loose dust as they disappeared into the commotion of the town.

Once the threat had passed, the Lockhart family slowly began to lower their weapons. One by one, the boys holstered their pistols. Clara, still alert, kept her eyes on the fading figures for a moment longer before lowering her shotgun back into its place under the tarp.

Woodrow gave a final glance around at his family, making sure all was well.

Then, in a voice that carried both relief and quiet authority, he said,

"Well, I believe we've had enough excitement for one day. Let's get out of this God-forsaken town."

Without hesitation, they climbed aboard the wagon and set out, the creak of wood and the jangle of harnesses filling the air as they made their way south toward the river.

The farther they traveled from the heart of town, the quieter it became. Within a short while, they could see the river glinting ahead, wide and strong under the deepening evening sky.

In the distance, the steamboat loomed larger with every step—the great vessel was already backed up against the dock, workers hurrying about to load cargo and usher passengers aboard.

As the wagon rolled closer to the dock, a man in a faded red vest stepped out from the wharf office and approached Woodrow.

The man eyed the wagon and the livestock and then asked,

"How many head of livestock you got? And how many people?"

Woodrow dismounted from his horse and motioned for the rest of the family to do the same. Standing tall, he answered,

"Well, sir, we've got one wagon, nineteen head of livestock, nine persons, and two hounds."

The dockworker gave a quick glance at the boys, who were straining to hear every word, and then smiled warmly at the ladies.

"Well, sir, it's two bits apiece for the livestock, two dollars for the wagon, and ten cents per person. That'll bring your total to seven dollars and sixty cents."

Without missing a beat, Woodrow reached into the small leather pouch he carried at his belt and drew out several gold coins. He counted them quickly, then handed over eight dollars.

"Well, sir," he said with a small nod, "Here's eight dollars. Keep the change, my friend."

The dockworker grinned broadly, tipping his hat again as he pocketed the coins.

"Much obliged, sir. We'll get you all boarded directly—wagon first, then the livestock."

With the deal settled, the Lockharts prepared to board the steamboat, eager to leave behind the dust, danger, and hard lessons of Memphis—and ready to face whatever lay waiting on the other side of the river.

Chapter 47
Crossing the Mighty Waters

The steamboat groaned against the pull of the mighty Mississippi, its great paddlewheel churning the river into a frothy wake as it carried the Lockharts—and all they owned—toward new beginnings.

The livestock was secured below, the wagon tied fast to the deck, and the family stood along the railing, watching in awe as the vessel powered through the wide, turbulent waters. Thick clouds loomed overhead, painting the sky a steely gray, but the children's laughter cut through the air like sunlight through the storm.

David leaned over the rail, pointing excitedly at the paddlewheel. Edward and Merle stood close by, eyes wide with wonder. Even Clara, who rarely let her guard down, allowed a small smile as she watched her children experience something entirely new.

Woodrow stood behind her, his arm wrapped firmly around her waist, his eyes scanning the broad river and the line of trees fading behind them on the eastern bank.

"This boat's got more power than I figured," Clara murmured.

Woodrow nodded.

"Tamed the Mississippi... at least a little."

She gave him a knowing look.

"Until the rain comes. Then even this big beauty'll be stuck in the mud like the rest."

Before Woodrow could reply, a voice called out.

"Sir?"

They turned to see the dock man approaching once more, tipping his hat.

"The captain asked if you wouldn't mind coming up to the wheelhouse, sir. Says he'd be honored to meet you."

Woodrow glanced at Clara.

"I'll be right back."

He made his way up the narrow staircase, boots thumping against the wooden steps. At the helm stood a man who looked like he'd been carved out of river rock himself— tall, broad-shouldered, with a thick white beard that reached his chest. A battered captain's hat sat on his head, and a long-stemmed pipe dangled from the corner of his mouth, releasing steady puffs of smoke into the air.

"Captain Walter James McCracken," he said, biting down on the stem of the pipe with a grin as wide as the river itself.

"Woodrow Lockhart," he replied, shaking the man's hand firmly.

"Well, Mr. Lockhart," the captain said with a chuckle, "When I saw that wagon board my boat with that big ol' mountain lion stretched across the top like a flag, I figured I had someone mighty interesting aboard. Word travels fast along the riverbanks, and your family's name... well, let's just say it's well known in these parts."

Woodrow gave a modest shake of his head.

"We didn't come looking for fame, Captain. Just trying to make our way west."

"Oh, I understand that," McCracken said with a wink. "But let me tell you, one of the stories I heard was that your middle boy killed that lion with nothin' but a Jim Bowie knife."

Woodrow chuckled.

"Well, he did finish it with the knife—but only after he shot the beast with one of those new Sharps military rifles. That slug went clean through the cat like it was tissue paper."

McCracken laughed, taking another puff of his pipe.

"That's more like it! I reckon the real story's even better than the tall tale."

Woodrow leaned against the window frame, sharing a few more details about the boys' target practice and how they'd all learned to shoot before setting off westward. The captain listened intently, nodding along with appreciation.

"Well, sir," he said at last, reaching out his hand again, "It's been my pleasure meetin' you. You and your family seem like good folk. I wish you the best—wherever this river, or the road beyond it, takes you."

Woodrow gave a firm handshake.

"Thank you, Captain. We sure do appreciate the passage."

As he made his way back down the stairs to his waiting family, the great river rolled on—wide, wild, and uncertain. But the Lockharts, for the first time in a long while, were not running. They were moving forward.

Together.

Steamboat Captain and Woodrow's meeting

Chapter 48
Into the Rough Land

The steamboat let out one last whistle as it eased away from the dock, leaving the Lockharts on solid ground once more. Woodrow tipped his hat and waved to Captain McCracken, who returned the gesture with a puff of his pipe and a wide grin from the wheelhouse.

Now, with their wagon reloaded and livestock gathered, the family turned their eyes westward.

Little Rock, Arkansas, lay ahead.

The landscape was already changing—dense thickets gave way to jagged hills and deep valleys. The terrain here was unlike anything they'd seen before, wild and untamed, marked with deep caves hidden in the folds of the earth. To some, they were marvels of nature. To others—like Woodrow—they were perfect hiding places for trouble.

Outlaws. Thieves. Men who'd rather take than earn.

He could almost hear the Marshal's warning echoing in his mind: "If there's a place that'll test your mettle, Lockhart, it's Arkansas."

Woodrow glanced around at his family, now seasoned travelers and well-armed defenders of their own fate. He had no doubt they'd face whatever came their way.

"Keep your eyes open," he muttered, more to himself than anyone else.

The path to Little Rock would take at least a week, if nothing slowed them down. But out here, delays were as common as dust. The old Military Road, carved through the hills, twisted and turned with no concern for wagon wheels or worn-out hooves. Each bend brought new challenges. One wrong turn or broken axle could leave them stranded in a land with no mercy.

The wagon creaked and groaned as it climbed yet another ridge. Every bump reminded them that everything they owned—every memory, every plan for the future—was packed inside that wooden box they now called home.

Clara kept a careful eye on the horses while Edward and Merle rode ahead to scout the trail. Ronald, quiet as always, sat beside his mother with his hand on the butt of his revolver. He might've been the youngest, but he was no child anymore.

Grass thinned as they dipped into the valleys, and Woodrow cursed under his breath. No grass meant hungry stock, and hungry stock meant slowed travel. He knew they'd need to push through these patches quickly before the animals grew too weak to carry on.

By the time the sun began to dip behind the distant ridgelines, the land around them had earned its reputation. Arkansas was not a place to take lightly. But the Lockharts weren't just passing through—they were surviving it.

And in just a few more days, they'd reach Fort Smith— the final town before Indian Territory. The last outpost of civilization before the real frontier began.

Woodrow rode silently, the weight of what lay ahead pressing down on him like the mountain air.

But still, they moved forward.

Because forward was the only way left to go.

Chapter 49
A Prayer at Sundown

Woodrow could feel it in his bones—they were close. The land had softened, flattened, and opened up with signs of settlement. Cabins dotted the hillsides, and wide pastures stretched out like a patchwork quilt. Just like the Marshal said, the closer they got to Fort Smith, the easier the land was to cross.

The sun was sinking fast, melting into the western ridgeline in a blaze of orange and gold. With dusk settling over the mountains, Ronald took the lead, guiding their faithful wagon toward a clearing he'd spotted up ahead. The boy had grown into a man on this journey, steady-handed and sure.

Woodrow kept pace alongside the draft horses, the true heroes of their trek. Through mud thicker than molasses, over rocks the size of water barrels, those beasts had never faltered. They were tired, but loyal. Just like the family they pulled.

By the time the wagon came to a stop, the clearing was bathed in the soft blue haze of evening. The women set to work quickly, preparing supper with a practiced rhythm. A fire crackled. The smell of fresh cornbread and hearty stew mingled with the sharp scent of brewing coffee. Clara had made something special—Woodrow could tell just by the richness in the air.

He breathed it in, deeply, a small smile tugging at the corner of his mouth. Hunger had been gnawing at him all day. Tonight, they'd eat like kings.

As everyone gathered around, the fire's glow flickering against their tired but contented faces, Woodrow turned to his only daughter, Mary. He gave her a gentle nod.

"Your turn, sweetheart," he said softly.

Mary looked to Clara, who nodded back with quiet encouragement. With hands folded and eyes cast upward, Mary's voice rang out, clear and true.

"Dear Father God, we thank You for Your Son who saved us from evil, and for keeping us fed through this journey going west. In Your only begotten Son's name, Jesus Christ... Amen."

A hush fell over the camp.

Woodrow's heart swelled with pride. Mary had never once complained on this long, uncertain road. She had been steady, graceful—a beam of light through every storm they faced.

Just as the family began to eat, a sound cut through the stillness.

A voice.

Faint.

Distant.

"In the camp… In the camp…"

Everyone froze.

The voice came again, echoing across the clearing like wind slipping through trees.

"In the camp…"

Woodrow rose slowly to his feet, one hand reaching for the rifle leaning against the wagon wheel. The others followed his lead, their eyes scanning the tree line, ears straining.

Who—or what was out there?

Dinner could wait.

Something had found them first.

Drinking coffee with Wild Bill Hickok

Chapter 50
Wild Bill at the Fire

The night had turned still—too still.

Woodrow stood firm, his Colt extended toward the shadows where the voice had come from. Beside him, his boys mirrored his stance, calm but ready, their guns steady in the flickering light of the campfire.

Then, out of the dark, the voice came again—clearer now, closer.

"Don't shoot! I'm a U.S. Marshal!"

A few tense seconds passed, and then a tall figure emerged from the tree line, hands raised in peace. His coat was dust-worn, and his boots were caked in the hard miles of the trail.

Woodrow stepped forward, lowering his weapon. He extended his hand, and the man took it with a firm shake.

"The name's William," the stranger said, "William 'Wild Bill' Hickok."

Woodrow's eyes widened.

He gave a respectful nod.

"Heard of you, sir. It's an honor."

"Pleasure's mine," Hickok replied, a tired but easy smile on his face.

"Didn't plan on stopping, but your coffees got a scent a man can't ignore—thought it was calling me down the trail."

Clara smiled quietly and poured a steaming tin cup, handing it to Woodrow, who passed it to the Marshal.

"You're welcome to join us," Woodrow said.

"There's stew and cornbread if you're hungry."

Hickok removed his hat, revealing long hair that shimmered in the firelight, longer even than Clara's or Mary's. He gave a nod of thanks. "I'd be obliged."

They made room for him by the fire, and as he took the first bite, his face relaxed.

"Been tracking a half-breed Osage outlaw—a dangerous man. Killed two of my deputies not three days back."

The camp fell silent.

He leaned in slightly, the firelight dancing in his weathered face.

"We had him. Deputies kept him tied up near a trading post while I went in for supplies. When I came back… the men were dead. Shot. Throats cut. Horses gone."

The silence deepened.

"I figure he stripped the bodies clean—guns, gold, gear—and vanished into the Arkansas wild."

Hickok shook his head slowly.

"He's likely halfway to Texas by now. Fast rider. Smarter than most.

Clara poured him another cup of coffee. The Marshal accepted it with a quiet nod, his eyes never leaving the dark horizon beyond the firelight.

After the meal, Hickok stood and dusted off his coat. He placed the hat back on his head and politely tipped it to Clara and Mary.

"Thank you for the kindness," he said.

"You've got a strong family, Mr. Lockhart. Stay alert out here. The man I'm tracking's a ghost in these woods— fast, mean, and desperate. If he comes around, he won't ask questions."

Woodrow stood and shook his hand once more.

"We'll be ready."

Without another word, Wild Bill Hickok vanished into the trees, swallowed by the night. The fire popped gently in his wake, and the stars above blinked down, silent witnesses to legends crossing paths.

Chapter 51
The Last Mile West

Woodrow and David sat beneath the dark sky, the fire a dim flicker between them. Neither spoke much—the quiet did most of the talking. Somewhere out in the black, an outlaw still roamed, and neither man intended to be caught off guard.

Clara, ever thoughtful, brought them a fresh pot of coffee just past midnight. The steam curled into the cold night air, carrying the rich scent that had once drawn Wild Bill Hickok straight from the trail. It helped keep their eyes open—and their minds sharp.

By dawn, the sun broke clean over the mountains, slicing through the mist like a promise. The night was over. They had made it through safely. As the warmth spread, so did their eagerness. Fort Smith was just ahead now, and Woodrow could feel it pulling him in like a magnet. He was ready.

Clara was already up, her hands busy making breakfast. The smell of fresh flapjacks filled the air, poured thick with molasses she'd picked up in the last town. It was the kind of morning that reminded you why the journey was worth it.

After breakfast, they hitched up the wagon. The horses moved with new energy, as if they too knew the end of the road was near.

When Fort Smith finally came into view, it felt like stepping into a different world. The town was bustling, complete with storefronts, stagecoaches, and signs swinging in the breeze. But there was something else, too—something dark.

A wooden sign arched over the main road, bold and chilling:

"Fifty Are Hanging at Noon Today!"

Clara saw it and turned to Woodrow, worry flickering in her eyes.

"Let's make this a short visit," she urged. "Get what we need before... before it begins."

He nodded.

"Agreed."

They moved quickly through the crowded streets, picking up supplies, asking questions, and gathering information. Townsfolk hurried along, their faces tense with anticipation. Justice, they called it. But to Clara, it felt more like a spectacle.

Before the clock struck noon, they had loaded the wagon and rolled out of town, leaving behind the sound of drums and the rising roar of the crowd as the hanging began.

Just beyond Fort Smith, they found a stream so clean and clear it looked like glass laid across the land. Ronald pulled the wagon up beside it, and the whole family worked together, filling barrels with the cold water. Even this small task felt sacred, like the land itself was welcoming them home.

They weren't going to Fort Gibson after all. Word from Wild Bill Hickok had confirmed what Woodrow feared— Fort Gibson was a ghost now, abandoned and forgotten, home only to a few scattered settlers.

But Hickok had told them something else—something better.

"There's a place farther west," he had said, "By the Arkansas River. The town's called Tulsa. Means 'Old Town' to the natives. Big water, rich land. Game in the hills. Good soil for planting. That's where your dreams will find ground to grow."

And so that was it.

Their course was set.

Tulsa.

The name rolled easy on the tongue, like a lullaby whispered in the dark.

They were a week away now. Just a week from laying down roots. A week of rest. A week from calling somewhere home.

The Indian Territory spread out before them, wide and wild and filled with possibility. The wind carried the promise of spring. The sky stretched out forever.

And with steady hearts and hopeful eyes, the Lockhart family pressed on—into the land of their destiny.

Driving the stock Westward

Chapter 52
A Land of Welcome

At last, they had arrived.

The Indian Territory stretched out before them like a dream freshly unrolled. After all the miles, the dangers, and the nights spent under uneasy stars, Woodrow and his family were finally here—on the land that might soon be home.

The trail before them twisted gently through a sea of green. Rolling hills shimmered under a clear blue sky, broken only by wide open clearings and grazing land that looked like it had been waiting just for them. The trail, Wild Bill Hickok had promised, would lead them straight to Tulsa. It was the best route west, he had said—lined with trading posts, friendly people, and military forts to keep the peace.

As the wagon creaked over a ridge, Woodrow spotted a settlement nestled alongside the road. It was unlike any they'd seen before. Teepees stood alongside wooden cabins, forming a patchwork village where two worlds seemed to meet.

A young Indian boy, no more than ten, stepped forward shyly, holding out beaded necklaces and feathers. Before anyone could speak, a tall man stepped in, gently moving the boy aside.

"Forgive him, sir," the man said with a nod.

"He gets eager to share our craft."

Woodrow smiled.

"No harm done. Say—do you have a store nearby?"

The man pointed toward a wooden building with a few horses tied at the hitching post out front.

"Right there, just past the stable."

Woodrow signaled to Ronald, and they guided the wagon toward the store. As they stopped, an old Indian man emerged from his teepee, his eyes fixed not on the family, but on the mountain lion's hide stretched across the top of the wagon.

He moved slowly, reverently, speaking in his own tongue and gesturing to the pelt. The man who'd welcomed them translated softly:

"He says the lion is sacred. The great cat is a guardian of family, of land. To bring down a lion is no small thing— it means strength, protection, and destiny. He wishes to honor the hunter."

Woodrow turned toward Edward and nodded.

"Get down, son."

Edward dismounted, unsure of what to expect. The old man took his hand and, with deep care, placed a necklace over his head. It was a hand-carved arrowhead, bound with an eagle feather, the leather cord dark and worn from age. The old man then swept his hand slowly through the air over

Edward's head and heart—once, twice, three times—blessing not just the boy, but all who traveled with him.

Edward lowered his head in gratitude.

"Thank you, sir."

The translator echoed his words in the native tongue, and the old man smiled.

While the moment settled into silence, Clara and Mary led the boys toward the general store, eager to replenish supplies. Meanwhile, Woodrow stayed behind to speak with the man who had first greeted them.

"Name's Jack B. Burns," the man said.

"You folks settlin' or passin' through?"

"We're headed for Tulsa," Woodrow replied.

Jack gave a knowing nod.

"Good choice. You're close—just two, maybe three days out, if the rivers behave. There's rafts fixed to ropes at the crossings. Not free, but they'll get you over in one piece."

Woodrow leaned in slightly.

"Any clean water nearby?"

Jack pointed down the road.

"Across from the stable, on your right. Cold, clear, and deep. Should do you just fine."

Woodrow tipped his hat in thanks and made his way toward the store.

Inside, Clara stood at a wooden counter, peering curiously into a large glass jar.

"What in the world you lookin' at?" Woodrow asked.

She grinned.

"Pickled buffalo tongues."

Woodrow raised an eyebrow.

"You enjoy that. I'll pass."

With a chuckle, he paid the shopkeeper and helped carry supplies to the wagon. The boys were already moving with practiced ease, loading the goods and getting ready for the road.

"All right, everyone," Woodrow called.

"Let's get to the well, fill them barrels, and be on our way."

With barrels full and spirits high, the wagon rolled forward once again. The sun shone down on the trail ahead, and the wind whispered through the trees.

Tulsa was near.

And with every creaking wheel and every hoofbeat on the earth, their dream came closer to becoming reality.

A Native Prayer

Chapter 53
The Land That Chose Them

Woodrow was really starting to admire the land they were traveling through as they continued westward. The hills were far easier to manage than the steep mountains they had struggled with earlier on their journey to the territory. The path now felt more welcoming—less like a challenge, more like a promise.

After crossing the last river, Woodrow recalled the man he'd spoken to there. A rugged figure, worn from travel, had mentioned it would be their final river crossing before reaching Tulsa. The Arkansas River, he had explained, ran alongside Tulsa and the nearby settlements. North of there, he said, was some of the finest farmland around, with abundant game, clean streams, and creeks perfect for fresh water. You could even dig your own wells if you liked.

The man's words stuck with Woodrow, echoing in his mind as the wagon creaked forward under the wide, open sky. Another day passed, and the family's excitement grew. Their destination was near.

Then, a sign came into view—weathered but unmistakable: Tulsa. Several trails split off from the main path, leading in different directions. Woodrow pulled back on the reins.

"Whoa!" he called out.

Ronald stopped just behind him, waiting quietly for further instructions from his pa.

Woodrow stood, surveying the land.

"Let's go north, men. I like what I see goin' that direction."

The trail they had been following split further ahead. One sign pointed toward a Trading Post. Another led toward Bird and Delaware Creeks. Woodrow, who always favored having water close to any place he'd call home, nodded firmly.

They turned toward the creeks.

What they found took their breath away.

Rolling hills rose gently to the west, natural shelters from future storms. The fields before them were open and wide, rich with pasture and farmland, more than enough to support a growing family. Clear water flowed nearby, and the soil looked deep and good.

They had found it.

"Home at last!" Woodrow shouted, turning toward his family, his voice full of emotion.

They had made it—all of them. No lives lost, no animals missing. They had come through every trial together.

And now, there was only one thing left to do.

As the wagon settled, Woodrow stepped forward and bowed his head.

"Thank you, God Almighty," he said, his voice steady.

"You have delivered us to our destiny without being harmed. You provided food and shelter, and all we can say now is—we thank You. In Your Son's name, Jesus Christ, *Amen.*"

Author's Thanks

I want to express my deepest appreciation to God and to my wife, who has been the cornerstone of my life for over forty-five years. Without her love, support, and unwavering presence, none of this would have been possible. She has been my rock since the day we met in high school.

Together, we've raised two wonderful children—our son, Derrick, and our daughter, Stephanie. Between them, we've been blessed with seven grandchildren, with another on the way.

Family has always been at the heart of everything we do. Our mother, who raised eight children—one daughter and seven sons—instilled in us the value that "God and Family are Forever." She reminded us that everything else in life fades in comparison. Her wisdom continues to guide us: keep your family close, and never go to bed angry, especially not with a loved one.

This storybook is a reflection of my childhood, the history of the Lockhart family, and the life experiences that have shaped me. It is a celebration of our journey and a tribute to the roots that have grounded us.

Thank you for being part of it.

Roger Dean Lockhart

www.ingramcontent.com/pod-product-compliance
Lightning Source LLC
Chambersburg PA
CBHW072117300726
48975CB00003B/844